IMAGINE THAT!

also edited by Sara and Stephen Corrin

PET STORIES FOR CHILDREN
THE FABER BOOK OF CHRISTMAS STORIES
ROUND THE CHRISTMAS TREE
ONCE UPON A RHYME: *101 Poems for Young Children*
THE FABER BOOK OF MODERN FAIRY TALES
STORIES FOR UNDER-FIVES
STORIES FOR SIX-YEAR-OLDS
STORIES FOR SEVEN-YEAR-OLDS
MORE STORIES FOR SEVEN-YEAR-OLDS
STORIES FOR EIGHT-YEAR-OLDS
STORIES FOR NINE-YEAR-OLDS
STORIES FOR TENS AND OVER
A TIME TO LAUGH: *Funny Stories for Children*
(Faber Paperback)

retold by Sara and Stephen Corrin
Illustrated by Errol Le Cain
MRS FOX'S WEDDING

ff

IMAGINE THAT!
Fifteen Fantastic Tales

Edited by
Sara and
Stephen Corrin

Illustrated by Jill Bennett

faber and faber
LONDON · BOSTON

First published in 1986
by Faber and Faber Limited
3 Queen Square, London WC1N 3AU

Photoset by Parker Typesetting Service, Leicester
Printed in Great Britain by
Butler & Tanner Ltd, Frome, Somerset
All rights reserved

British Library Cataloguing in Publication Data

Imagine that! : fifteen fantastic tales.
1. Tales
I. Corrin, Sara   II. Corrin, Stephen
III. Bennett, Jill, *1934–*
398.2'1   PZ8.1
ISBN 0–571–13843–8

Library of Congress Cataloging in Publication Data

Corrin, Sara.
Imagine that!
Summary: Presents a collection of traditional tales about magical events
from various parts of the world.
1. Tales.   [1. Folklore]   I. Corrin, Stephen.
II. Bennett, Jill, ill.   III. Title.
PZ8.1.C788Im   1986   398.2   86-2164
ISBN 0–571–13843–8

for Phyllis

Contents

Acknowledgements

We are grateful to the undermentioned authors, publishers and agents for permission to include the following:

'Two Greedy Bears' by James Reeves, reprinted by permission of Hamish Hamilton Ltd. and the James Reeves Estate.

'Arap Sang and the Cranes' and 'Onsongo and the Masai Cattle' from *Tales Told near a Crocodile* and 'Chura and Marwe' from *Tales Told to an African King*, by Humphrey Harman, published by Hutchinson Publishing Group Ltd.

'The Popplesnitch' from *The Amber Mountain* by Agnes Szudek, reprinted by permission of the author and Tessa Sayle.

'The Black Thief' by Eileen O'Faolain, reprinted by permission of the author.

'The Clever Peasant Girl' from *Salt and Gold* by Marie Burg, published by Blackie and Son Ltd.

'Volkh's Journey to the East' from *The Knights of the Golden Table* by E. M. Almedingen, reproduced by permission of The Bodley Head.

'The Living Kuan-Yin' from *Sweet and Sour* by C. Kendall, reproduced by permission of The Bodley Head.

'Arion and the Dolphin' from *To Read and to Tell* by Norah Montgomerie, reproduced by permission of The Bodley Head.

We are much indebted to the many school librarians and children's librarians who have been so readily forthcoming in helping us with our enquiries.

This book is entitled *Imagine That*! but it would be impossible for us to imagine its coming into being without the sagacious guidance at every stage of Phyllis Hunt, our editor at Faber and Faber.

Foreword

We once knew a lady whose eyebrows were permanently raised. We used to refer to her as P. B. (standing for Perpetual Bewilderment). We certainly expect this collection to raise your eyebrows an inch or two higher than usual, but perhaps P. W. (Perpetual Wonderment) would be a more appropriate description for you as you read or listen to these fabulous tales.

All but one of the stories – *Belinda and Bellamant* – are probably immensely ancient, and you could well be one among the thousandth generation now enjoying them. Such magical tales rise from somewhere deep, quite unfathomably deep, in man's imagination and they seem to spring from every country, every people, the world over. In the words of the famous scholar Paul Hazard, 'children's stories keep alive a sense of nationality, but they also keep alive a sense of humanity; they convey with deep love their feelings for their native land but they also describe faraway lands where unknown brothers live . . . Every country gives and every country receives . . . Thus in our impressionable years the Universal Republic of childhood is born.' (This may sound a wee bit awesome, but it contains a deep, undying truth.)

We wish you joy in reading – or hearing – these tales: exciting and beautiful African stories; funny stories from Lithuania, Czechoslovakia, Italy and Persia; a typical Irish legend from guess where; a heroic tale from Russia; a touching tale from Greece; a thought-provoking legend from China; and from our own Edith Nesbit the enchanting *Belinda and Bellamant*.

Wise Sorfarina

an Italian tale
retold by Jan Vladislav

Sorfarina was a girl as beautiful as she was wise. She not only knew how to read and write, but she also did all sums in her head and could speak ten different languages. She was her teacher's favourite pupil, and this was a great honour for her, since it was a school attended not only by the sons of wealthy merchants and noblemen, but also by the son of the king himself. Yet Sorfarina was by far the best pupil of them all, and their teacher held her up as an example to the others. And whenever he had to leave the class for any reason, it was Sorfarina whom he entrusted to keep order.

As was only natural, some of her fellow-pupils resented this; for who had ever heard of a mere merchant's daughter giving orders to the sons of noblemen – even to the prince who was to inherit the throne? Thus, whenever the teacher left the classroom and put Sorfarina in his place behind his desk, the pupils started misbehaving themselves, most of all the prince. Time

and again Sorfarina urged him to be quiet and attend to his work, but he only shook his head stubbornly, saying he was a prince and did not have to obey anybody.

'So you won't obey me?' Sorfarina said to him one day, her patience exhausted.

'No, I will not!' the prince retorted.

'We shall see,' said Sorfarina angrily, and she slapped the prince on the face.

Now this was quite a new experience for the prince and he stopped making a nuisance of himself, never again giving Sorfarina cause for annoyance. But he did not forget the slap she had given him.

Sorfarina soon forgot all about it. The days and the weeks and the months passed, year followed year, and before the merchant knew it, his daughter was a beautiful young lady, and he decided that it was time he found her a husband.

The prince had grown up too, and he no longer went to school but rode out to hunt and fight in tournaments. Before the king knew it, his son was a handsome young man, and he decided that it was time he found him a wife.

'My son, it is time you were married,' the king told him one day.

'Certainly, if that is your wish,' the prince replied, 'but I shall only marry the wise Sorfarina.'

'Sorfarina?' said the king in astonishment. 'But she comes from a merchant's family, and you are a prince. You ought to choose a different bride.'

'No, Father,' the prince insisted, 'I shall only marry Sorfarina and no one else.'

The king saw that his son's mind was made up, and he sent for the merchant.

'What is it you desire of me, Your Majesty?' asked the merchant, bowing low before the king on his throne.

'Get up and come closer, my dear merchant,' said the king. 'My son has taken it into his head to marry your daughter, Sorfarina. What do you say about this?'

'Why, what should I say?' said the merchant. 'If that is what your son wants, and if my daughter agrees, let them get married by all means. But, perhaps I ought to remind Your Majesty that Sorfarina is only a merchant's daughter and your son is a prince. Ought he not to marry a princess rather than my daughter?'

'That is exactly what I told him,' said the king, 'but he will not hear of any other bride. So let them get married! I do not mind!'

'Well, why not?' replied the wise Sorfarina. 'I shall take him, even though he did annoy me at school. Perhaps he won't annoy me any more.'

A royal wedding was soon being prepared, and Sorfarina's family got together all the clothing and linen that she would need. In the royal palace preparations were made for a great feast, to which all the noblemen and merchants in the city were invited.

The feast lasted for three days and three nights, during which time immense quantities of food were eaten and much wine was drunk. At the end of the three days the guests left for their homes, and the prince and his bride retired to their rooms. As soon as they were alone the prince locked the door, put the key in his pocket and said to his wife:

'Do you remember, Sorfarina, how we used to go to school together?'

'Yes, I remember,' replied Sorfarina.

'And do you remember how you used to keep order in class when the teacher had to go away?'

'Yes, I remember.'

'And do you remember how one day you slapped my face?'

'Yes, I remember,' said Sorfarina for the third time, and she laughed merrily at the recollection.

But the prince was not laughing; on the contrary, he looked very angry.

'Do you regret it?' the prince asked further.

'No, I don't!' cried Sorfarina. 'I don't regret it in the least, and I never shall. And if need be, I shall slap you again!'

'Oh, you will, will you!' exclaimed the prince. 'In that case you are going to sleep on the floor.'

And he went to bed, while his bride had to lie down on the floor.

Sorfarina did not mind, however. She rested her head on her elbow, turned her face to the wall, and was soon fast asleep.

The prince felt sorry for her. Although he was still annoyed about the way she had slapped him, he was genuinely in love with her.

At about midnight he called out to her:

'Sorfarina, are you asleep?'

'Yes, I am,' replied Sorfarina.

'Now do you regret slapping me?'

'No, I don't,' said Sorfarina again. 'I don't regret it in the least, and never shall. And if need be I shall slap you again!'

'Oh, so that is how you feel, is it?' exclaimed the prince. 'In that case you are going to sleep outside the door.'

And saying this he pushed Sorfarina out of the room. Sorfarina did not mind; curling herself up on the threshold, she rested her head on her elbow and was soon fast asleep once more.

The prince again felt sorry for her. Although he was angry about that slap she had given him, he was truly in love with her, and in the morning he came and asked:

'Sorfarina, are you asleep?'

'Yes, I am,' Sorfarina replied.

'And do you regret slapping my face?'

'No, I don't regret it, and I never shall!' retorted Sorfarina. 'And if need be I shall slap you again!'

'Oh, shall you indeed!' exclaimed the prince. 'I'll teach you a lesson! You are going to sleep in the dungeon.' And with these words he caught her by the hand, dragged her off to the dungeon and locked her in.

Sorfarina did not mind, though. When evening came, she stretched herself out on the straw, rested her head on her elbow and was soon fast asleep again.

In the morning the prince came to the little window in the door of her cell and said:

'Well, Sorfarina, do you now regret slapping my face?'

But Sorfarina was even more stubborn than the prince himself.

'No, I don't regret it, and I never shall,' she said. 'And I promise you I shall slap you again.'

'All right,' replied the prince. 'When you do, I shall forgive you for that first slap. But until then you will stay in the dungeon, living on bread and water. I, for my part, am going abroad. I leave for Rome tomorrow.'

'Have a good time,' said Sorfarina, and the prince left. As soon as he had gone she started to scratch away at the wall with a long needle, and she went on doing this until she had made a hole in the thick stone wall. Looking out through the hole, she saw her father's clerk passing by.

'Hullo there, Mr Thomas!' she called out to him. 'Come over here, please!'

The poor man could not make out where the voice was coming from, and he turned about on the spot like a weathercock.

'Who is calling me?' he asked.

'It is me – Sorfarina! Here in the dungeon. Please send my father to me.'

The merchant came running at once, frightened by the news of his daughter's imprisonment.

'What has happened to you, Sorfarina? How did you come to be here?' he asked her.

'Do not worry about me,' Sorfarina soothed him. 'I intend to get out of here as soon as I can, and you must help me. Have an underground passage dug from our garden, and I shall see to the rest.'

The merchant had a lot of money and was therefore able to have things done quickly. The passage was finished within a day and a night, and Sorfarina was soon free again. She packed a box full of her best clothes, took some money with her and, boarding her father's fastest ship, sailed straight for Rome.

She arrived there on the same day as her husband, found out where he was staying, and rented a palace opposite. Putting on a fine dress which he had never seen her wear before, she sat down by an open window.

In a little while the prince came past and he stopped in the street, gazing up at her in surprise. The beautiful lady at the

window looked exactly like his wife, and if he had not known that she was in a dungeon in Palermo he would have sworn that this was indeed Sorfarina. He at once sent a servant to her with a message.

'Noble lady,' the servant said, bowing before her, 'my master, the Prince of Palermo, would like to call on you at your convenience.'

'I shall be pleased to receive him,' Sorfarina replied.

So the prince came to visit Sorfarina, bowing courteously and sitting down next to her before he started speaking.

'Do you know that you resemble a certain lady in my native Palermo? If I did not know it was impossible, I would think you were one and the same person.'

Sorfarina laughed and said:

'But, my dear sir, did you not know that there are seven of us all told who resemble each other like so many eggs?'

The prince could not take his eyes off the beautiful lady.

'Are you single?' he asked her at last.

'As you are,' replied Sorfarina with a smile.

'And would you like to get married?'

'Only if I could marry a prince like you,' said Sorfarina, laughing once more.

The prince started to call on her every day, bringing her flowers and sending her gifts. Within a week they were married, and a year and a day later a son was born to them.

'What name shall we give him?' asked the prince.

'He was born in Rome, so let us call him Roman,' decided Sorfarina.

Before long, however, the prince remembered his wife in the dungeon at Palermo, and he said to his Roman wife:

'I must go home, my dear. My father has written to me, asking me to come and help him govern his kingdom.'

'Yes, of course,' replied Sorfarina, 'but do come back soon, for who else is there to look after our little Roman?'

The prince therefore bade farewell to his wife and son and left for Palermo. Sorfarina lost no time either. As soon as the prince's coach had vanished round the first bend, she boarded her father's fastest ship with her son, and reached Palermo on the same day as her husband.

The prince went straight to the dungeon. Opening the door he found Sorfarina sitting there quite happily, as though he had only been gone a day and not over a year.

The prince felt very sorry for her. Although he was angry about the slap she had given him, he still loved her dearly.

'Well now, Sorfarina, do you regret slapping me?'

But Sorfarina would not give in.

'No, I do not regret it, and never shall,' she said. 'When the time comes I shall slap you again!'

'All right,' replied the prince angrily. 'When you do that, I shall forgive you for the first slap. But until then you will stay here in the dungeon, living on bread and water. I, for my part, am going abroad. I leave for Genoa tomorrow.'

'Have a good time,' replied Sorfarina.

As soon as the prince had gone she slipped out through the underground passage. Leaving her little son with her parents, she took some money, and boarded her father's ship again, this time sailing for Genoa.

She arrived on the same day as the prince. As soon as her servants had discovered where the prince was staying she rented a magnificent palace just opposite, put on her finest clothes, which the prince had never seen her wear before, and sat down at an open window.

After a little while, the prince happened to walk past the palace, and he stopped in the street, gazing up at the window in disbelief. The beautiful lady he saw there looked exactly like his wife in Palermo and his wife in Rome.

'If I did not know that one was in a dungeon at Palermo and the other with our son in Rome, I could swear that it was one and the same face,' he said to himself, sending a servant to the lady with his message.

'Greetings, noble lady, from my master, the Prince of Palermo. He would like to make your acquaintance,' said the servant, bowing before Sorfarina, who replied:

'Let him come, by all means.'

The prince could not take his eyes off the beautiful lady, who looked even more like Sorfarina, now that he saw her close up.

'Do you know that you resemble a lady in Palermo and another in Rome?' he asked her.

Sorfarina laughed and said:

'Surely, my dear sir, you have heard that there are seven of us in the world, each one just like the other?'

'Are you single?' asked the prince.

'No, I am a widow, just like you,' Sorfarina replied, smiling.

'And would you like to marry again?'

'Not unless I could find a man such as you,' said Sorfarina, smiling secretly to herself once more.

The prince now started calling on his beautiful neighbour every day, bringing her flowers and sending her gifts. Within a week he had proposed to her, and within a year and a day a little boy was born to them.

'What shall we call him?' asked the prince.

'Let us call him Genoan, since he was born in Genoa,' replied Sorfarina.

Shortly afterwards the prince remembered his wife, whom he had left in the dungeon at Palermo.

'I have to go home, my dear,' he told Sorfarina. 'My father has written, asking me to come.'

'Go by all means if you must,' replied Sorfarina, 'but come back soon, or else who will look after our little Genoan?'

The prince therefore returned home to Palermo, and so did Sorfarina, who arrived on the same day as he did.

The prince went straight to the dungeon, only to find

Sorfarina sitting there as if he had been away a mere day, and not over a year.

The prince felt sorry for her. Though he still could not forgive her for slapping his face he loved her with all his heart.

'Tell me, Sorfarina,' he said, 'do you regret that you slapped me?'

But Sorfarina was really stubborn.

'No, I do not regret it, and never shall,' she replied. 'And when the time comes I shall slap you again!'

'All right,' cried the prince in great vexation. 'When you do, I shall forgive you for that first slap. But until then you will stay here in the dungeon, living on bread and water. As for me, I am going abroad. I leave for Alexandria tomorrow.'

'Have a good time,' said Sorfarina as they parted. As soon as the prince had gone, she left the dungeon by her underground passage and got ready for a journey. She sailed in her father's fastest ship for Alexandria, leaving her little son Genoan with her parents and with his brother Roman.

In Alexandria Sorfarina married the prince for the fourth time. For again, she took a palace opposite his residence, again she surprised him by looking so much like his other wives; again she accepted his courtship and his offer of marriage, and again a child was born to them within a year and a day. This time it was a little girl.

'What shall we call her?' asked the prince.

'Why, let us call her Alexandra, since she was born in Alexandria,' suggested Sorfarina.

But once more the prince did not stay with his wife and child very long, for he again remembered his first wife in Palermo and felt he must go and see her.

'I must go home,' he told his Alexandrian wife. 'My father has sent for me.'

'That being so, there is nothing we can do about it,' said Sorfarina. 'But come back soon, won't you, so that our daughter is not without her father for too long.'

The prince promised this and set out on his journey. When he arrived in Palermo he went straight to the dungeon, but again

Sorfarina was already there, waiting for him. The prince felt sorry for her, and although he could not help being angry about the way she had slapped him, he still loved her best of all his wives.

'Tell me, Sorfarina, do you at last regret slapping me?' he asked.

But Sorfarina would not give in.

'No, I do not regret it, and never shall,' she said. 'And when the time comes I shall slap you again. It will be very soon now.'

This infuriated the prince, who cried:

'All right! When you do, I shall forgive you for the first slap. But you had better hurry, for within a week I shall marry again, taking an English princess for my wife. After that it will be too late!'

And with these words he left her.

This had not been a vain threat, either. He sent fast couriers to the King of England, asking for the hand of his daughter. Within a week, the king and queen as well as the princess were already in Palermo, and preparations were afoot for the royal wedding.

But the wedding did not take place. When all the guests had assembled in the royal palace and the prince with his English bride was about to leave the throne hall at the head of the wedding procession, a beautiful lady wearing a queen's robes suddenly appeared in the palace, carrying a baby girl in her arms and with two handsome little boys at her side.

The courtiers all gasped in astonishment, for surely this was none other than the wise Sorfarina, their prince's wife!

'Roman and Genoan,' the lady said to her two sons, 'go and kiss your father's hand.'

Only now did the prince realize that this was his Roman, Genoan and Alexandrian wife.

'So this is the slap in the face you have been promising me,' he cried, blushing a deep red as he kissed his children – the two little boys and little Alexandra.

Thus did Sorfarina triumph. But the prince was no longer angry with her, for he saw that she was really wise, and that he had deserved the treatment she had meted out to him.

As for the English princess, she left as she had come, without a bridegroom or a husband. She would not again wish, as long as she lived, to marry the Prince of Palermo.

The wise Sorfarina, on the other hand, was well satisfied with the prince. In the course of time she gave him seven children, all of them looking exactly alike, just like those seven beauties which she had talked about when the prince had courted her in Rome, Genoa and Alexandria.

Two Greedy Bears

by James Reeves

In long-ago Persia there lived two bears. One was called Lal, and his sister was called Kara. They were small, brown and furry. They played in a forest on the side of a mountain. Best of all, they loved to find sweet things to eat. Lal would climb a pomegranate tree and throw down the sweet, juicy fruit. Kara, who was just as nimble as her brother, would scamper up a fig tree and gather as many ripe figs as she could lay her paws on. Then together they would have a feast – they would eat up every scrap of the fruit and finish by licking the juice from each other's furry coats.

Lal and Kara were fond of nuts and berries too. They were still fonder of the honey of the wild bees. They scooped it out of hollow trees, sometimes getting their paws stung. In short, they were very greedy little bears. They even took to going down to the nearby town of Allarcand, at the bottom of the mountain, and robbing the gardens of their ripe peaches, apricots and oranges. They were careful not to be caught.

But then something happened.

It so chanced that on the edge of Allarcand lived a clever wood-carver named Morad. All day he worked in his workshop, making wooden figures for rich merchants and simple furniture for the poorer people; his carvings of animals such as tigers and bears, geese and wild swans were very much in demand. A life-sized carving of a two-hundred-year-old tortoise brought him some fame and a good deal of money. Often he went out with his saws, his hammer and his chisels to his neighbours' houses to do all the jobs that needed to be done almost every day of the week. He was known throughout the town for his skill in fixing up kitchen shelves or loosening a cupboard door that had got stuck. Morad had no children, but he lived snugly enough in his wooden house with its pool in the back garden and a few trees to give him fruit and shade.

Once a month Morad had to go into the big city, seven miles from Allarcand, to deliver some important piece of carving he had been ordered to make, to adorn the walls in a rich merchant's house. He did not greatly enjoy these journeys, for he was short and inclined to be stout, and the long dusty road made him tired and out of breath. But there were rich men in the city, and Morad was paid good money for the work they ordered. Now one day he was in the main square of the city, where he had just collected from several of his customers a large bag of gold and silver pieces, which hung at his belt. He sat down on a bench in the shade of a palm-tree, drinking sherbet out of a stoneware cup because of the heat of the day. He caught sight of his friend, Yussef the goldsmith.

'Allah be praised!' said Morad. 'What brings you to the city, friend Yussef? The eyes of this person are as glad to behold you as are the eyes of a traveller through the desert to see the roofs of his native town.'

'The eyes of this person,' answered Yussef, 'are similarly gladdened to behold you, friend Morad. If you consider me worthy, I will sit down at your side in the shade and take a cup of sherbet with you. This throat is as dry as the bed of a river before the rainy season.'

The two men sat together in the shade. Unlike Morad, who was short and round, Yussef was tall and thin. He had a narrow black beard and deep-set eyes. He wore a grey woollen gown, with a pocket on either side. Just now Yussef's eyes rested on the money-bag at Morad's belt.

'Like you, my friend,' he said, 'I also have come to the city to collect money from those who have bought my wares. What excellent judgement they have, I cannot help thinking. No goldsmith in all Persia makes prettier rings for the merchants to put on the fingers of their wives. Today I delivered a pair of silver

dishes in the shape of swans with outspread wings to the Kazir himself. Ah, if you could have heard his cries of delight, my friend, it would have rejoiced your heart. I am in a fair way of business, but it is hard work and I am always at it, night and day.' Here Yussef sighed deeply, as if to show how tiring his work was, and took a draught of his cooling drink.

'I too have my customers,' Morad said, 'for has it not been said, "Where there is work for the hatter, is there not also work for the shoemaker?" '

So the two friends talked on, sipping their sherbet, until the sun began to sink behind the mosques and minarets of the city. Morad was thinking of the seven long miles he had to trudge home before darkness fell.

'Come, friend Yussef,' he said, 'it is time for us to go home. In the words of the immortal sage, "There is a time to drink and

26

rest the spirit: there is a time to leave off drinking and urge the weary feet upon the homeward road.'' It would be an ill thing if we were to be overtaken by the shades of night before we reach home.'

'You are right, friend Morad,' agreed Yussef. 'I have heard that there are thieves abroad, and they must not be allowed to find two honest traders in the open fields after dark.'

So off they went. The short form of Morad was obliged some-times to trot beside his long-legged companion. They took the road to Allarcand. They walked together in silence for some miles. Then Morad uttered a long sigh and said:

'I fear, my friend, that I must ask you to pause with me at the roadside for a few minutes. I am weary. The Prophet, who knows and ordains all things, has not provided me with a walking apparatus as well designed as yours.'

'Very well,' agreed Yussef. 'Has it not been said that if the dromedary would travel with the tortoise, he must shorten his pace?'

Morad drew himself up and looked hurt.

'I am no tortoise, my friend,' he said. 'But I shall be glad to rest.'

In the broad shadow of a cedar tree they sat down for a few minutes at the roadside. Then on they trudged, making as good speed as they could. To Morad the road seemed to get longer as they journeyed. Long before the minarets of Allarcand came into view, the armies of darkness had begun their swift descent upon the land.

'It is not safe, friend Morad,' said Yussef, pulling at his long beard, 'to carry our money-bags any further tonight. In that field grows an ancient fig tree with wide-spreading roots. I have used it before to hide some of my wares when I feared that thieves were lurking to rob me. Do you not think it prudent to leave our money beneath those roots? There it will be safe. In the morning we can meet together and recover it.'

'Undoubtedly you are right,' said Morad. 'In the words of the sage, "There is a time to copy the boldness of the lion, and a time to imitate the wisdom of the serpent." Let us do as you say, and no sooner will the golden riders of the day put to flight the armies of darkness than we shall meet each other beside this fig tree, refreshed by a deep draught from the wine-barrel of sleep.'

'So be it,' said Yussef. 'Let us waste no more of the declining day, but act with resolution.'

They hurried to the field of the fig tree and, after looking round to see that none observed them, they pushed their bags deep beneath the roots.

Then the goldsmith and the woodcarver took the road for Allarcand. Yussef lived on the nearer side of the town and Morad at the far side. They parted outside Yussef's house. When they did so, the stars were shining in the sky, and most of the good people of the town had gone to bed. Only loafers and malefactors lingered in the narrow alleys, and all was silent except for the barking of a restless dog here and there and the chattering of monkeys high in the palm trees.

At dawn Yussef awoke. As soon as he had said his prayers, he immediately thought of his money under the fig tree. As he put on his woollen gown, a cunning thought struck him. Is it not written in the Book of Wisdom that the light that is reflected from a gold piece may dazzle the eye of virtue?

'What does friend Morad want with all that money?' he said to himself. 'He has a snug house and a nice place of business. He has a pretty garden in which to rest himself in the heat of the day. He has no wife and children to feed and clothe. But my wife is always demanding new gowns and my little boy and girl – may Allah bless their merry hearts and their brown eyes! – are for ever clamouring for food, for toys and sweetmeats from the market. I would not be without them for the world, but no man can deny that they are as an ever-yawning hole in my purse. Is it not written that those who have plenty should come to the aid of the poor and needy? Morad must come to the aid of his friend. I will hurry out and see if I cannot get some of Morad's winnings as well as my own.'

Now Yussef lived on the side of the town nearest to the field of the fig tree. It did not take him long to reach it. No one was in sight, for as yet the golden fingers of dawn scarce pointed to the tops of the minarets. Quickly he knelt at the foot of the tree, felt beneath the spreading roots and drew out both his and Morad's leather bags. Now, he had meant to take only one or two gold pieces from his friend's bag, but at that very instant he heard the jingling of bells. This meant only only thing – the near approach of a camel train. Hurriedly he stuffed the whole bag into one of his deep pockets. Into the other pocket he thrust his own bag and turned homewards. Gathering the skirts of his gown about his knees, he walked as fast as his long shanks would carry him.

In his house at the top of the town Morad slept late. The hurried tramp back from the city the day before had wearied him. The sun was already high when the windows of sleep opened to permit his eyes the sight of day. At once Morad thought of the money under the fig tree, where he had agreed to meet Yussef. Hastily refreshing himself with a cup of coconut milk and robing himself for the journey, he hurried through the town and reached the field somewhat out of breath.

Yussef, who had had plenty of time to return home and leave the money-bags in a safe place under his work bench, had been on the lookout for his friend. Coming out of his house just as Morad had passed, he soon caught up with him.

'Greetings, my friend,' he said. 'The blessings of the Prophet upon you. May he smile on you and your concerns this day and always. Let us at once recover our money and return home. You are smaller than I. Let it be you who stoops under the tree and lays hands upon the bags.'

Morad did as he was told. For a long time he fumbled and at length stood up with a look of consternation on his honest face.

'The bags are not there,' was all he said.

'Not there?' repeated Yussef with well-feigned incredulity.

'They are not there,' repeated Morad. 'A thief has been here before us.'

'Let me see for myself,' said Yussef. He lifted up the skirt of his robe and knelt down, groping under the roots. Then he stood up, his face scarlet with anger and amazement.

'Yes,' he spluttered, 'a thief has certainly been here, and you know well who it is. Only you and I know where the money was. Admit it, Morad. You were out before me, and have already been here and taken the bags. Ah, my friend, how have I deserved this treatment? But perhaps the devil of greed entered your heart and prompted your hand to do wrong by your friend. Give me back my bag, and I will forgive you and say no more about it. I will forgive you, may Allah do likewise. All the same I am grieved. Is it not written in the Book of Wisdom that a man may as soon trust a friend as the stray dog he has brought into his house for pity and given food from his own larder? Both may turn and rob their benefactor.'

Yussef pretended to be deeply hurt. Morad, who could not help wondering in what way Yussef had been his benefactor, protested his innocence. He told Yussef that he had not been near the fig tree since they had both left it the night before. He said he would as soon speak ill of Allah himself as steal from his friend. Yussef knew this very well. All Morad's protestations were in vain.

'Well,' said the cunning goldsmith, 'if what you say is true, it must be some nocturnal vagabond who has been here before us. It seems, friend Morad, as if we have both lost our money. I will go and make a complaint to the chief magistrate, and doubtless the thief will be caught. Now I must go home. I have work to do, to make up for the loss of my earnings.'

Yussef hurried off, and Morad turned slowly homewards, thinking hard as he went.

'I am afraid,' he told himself, 'that there is only one person who can have taken that money. It is Yussef himself. Is it not written that a man may as soon trust his friend as the snake that comes to drink from his pool. Well, I will think of a way to get that money back. Even an honest man must sometimes be crafty if he is to keep what is his.'

31

Now Morad had noticed that the fence at the back of his garden had been broken away. Looking out of his window one night when the silver bowl of the moon was full to the brim, he had seen two brown, furry bear-cubs pushing their way through the gap and stealing his ripe plums. He had not yet had time to repair the gap, and this gave him an idea. He determined to capture Lal and Kara next time they came – for it was indeed those two greedy cubs who had been robbing his orchard. He dug a deep pit in the garden near the gap in the fence. He covered it with a network of thin willow branches. Over these he spread broad fig-leaves, and on top of these he laid fat, juicy peaches and bunches of tempting grapes.

'This should help me catch those greedy bears,' he said. 'Has it not always been seen that the wit of man is more than a match for the strength of the beast?'

Sure enough, that very night, there was a rustling at the end of the garden, a scuffling of paws, and then a thud. This was followed by squeaks of alarm from the two little bears, who, tempted by the sweet-smelling peaches and grapes, had tumbled into the pit. As they tried vainly to scramble out, Morad hurried up with a strong net, like those used by fishermen on the waters of the Caspian. He threw it right over Lal and Kara and had little difficulty in hauling them out of the pit, safe and sound but scared out of their small, furry lives. He carried them into the house. In their fright they clung together, wondering what was going to happen to them. They had no cause for fear, for Morad was the kindest of men and had never harmed a living creature, not even a poisonous snake he had once found curled up among the shavings under his bench. He shut the cubs in a little room with a barred window, leading out of his workshop. He left them milk and fruit and honey-buns. Soon they felt quite at home and had almost forgotten their alarming experience.

In the morning the woodcarver set to work to build a life-sized model of the goldsmith. He carved a head from a big piece of soft wood. He shaped the eyes, nose and mouth, and from the chin he hung a black beard made of goat-hair. He mounted this on a rough wooden frame and dressed the figure in a grey gown with a girdle of cord and two deep side pockets. He left it standing in his workshop. Then he went into his garden and gathered ripe peaches and pears. Next he fetched sweet cakes from the larder. These he put into the pockets of the gown and the wooden hands of the image of Yussef. Very quickly the bears learned to get their food, not from Morad, but from the carved figure. How

they enjoyed nuzzling in its pockets and its wooden hands for the sweetmeats they loved so much! How they squeaked with delight as they guzzled the fruit and cakes which were so much more exciting than anything they had found in the forest! After three days they scarcely gave a thought to their anxious parents, but began to love the wooden image just as if it were their own father.

'So far, so good,' said Morad. 'I have trained my two little friends well. May Allah, who can bring about all things, see that my friends repay me by helping me in the rest of my plan.'

Now we must turn to Yussef the goldsmith and the family who cost him so much to feed and clothe. His two little children were Bahram, an active, merry boy of eight, and Soriyah, a girl of seven. They played together in the fields and woods and in the streets of Allarcand. Sometimes they quarrelled, as brothers and sisters will, but usually they were the best of friends, for Soriyah adored her brother and was always ready to do what he suggested. Everyone in Allarcand was their friend, for they greeted all alike with their happy smiles and bubbling chatter. They often called on Morad the woodcarver, who would sometimes stop in his work to make them a tiny boat to sail on his pool or shower them with wood shavings which tickled them till they rolled over, laughing.

A day or two after he had tamed the bear-cubs, Morad found Bahram and Soriyah standing at the door of his workshop. They looked as if they would like to be invited in.

'Ah,' thought the woodcarver, 'Allah has answered my prayer.'

He laid down his tools and said:

'Why, hallo! If it isn't young Bahram and Soriyah. What brings you here? Perhaps someone has told you I have just been to the market to buy sugar-plums and that delicious sweet you love so much, made of honey, almonds and sesame. Come inside and try some.'

The children's eyes sparkled. Soon they were munching the rich sweetmeat with feelings like those of a good soul tasting the sweets of paradise after a virtuous and useful life.

Bahram said, when he could eat no more:

'Thank you, Morad. Yours are the best sweets in all Allarcand. Now it is time we were going home. Mother will be wondering where we are.'

But Morad had shut and bolted the door. Now he said:

'How would you like to stay with me, my dears? Your father owes me a lot of money, and perhaps you can help him to pay it back. Wouldn't you like to do that?'

He spoke gently, but little Soriyah was scared and began to cry. Bahram tried to comfort her, saying that Morad was their friend and everything would be all right. But he looked rather solemn and all the laughter had left his brown eyes.

'Don't be afraid,' Morad said kindly. 'I will send a message to your father and mother to tell them where you are. Look here. I have the neatest little room for you to stay in.' He took each of them by the hand and led them up a narrow stair at the back of the kitchen. They went into a small room at the top of the house. There was a little window overlooking the garden, and the room smelt of new wood. There was a thick rug on the floor. Morad said he would give the children supper, and they could spend the night there. The children, thinking it was all rather an adventure, liked the little room and soon felt at home.

'Isn't it fun,' said Bahram. 'It will be something to tell every-one about, won't it?'

Next Morad put sweets and honey-cakes into the pockets of the image and let Lal and Kara out of the room at the back of the workshop. The bear-cubs scampered up to the image and found the sweets and cakes with their brown furry paws. Of course he did not let the children know that Lal and Kara were in the same house, or they would have wondered what he was up to. Perhaps, too, Soriyah might have been scared.

Then Morad went out of the house, locking the door behind him. He took a leisurely stroll in the streets of Allarcand, as many did in the cool of the evening. Along the narrow lanes he sauntered, until he came to the great open place in the middle of the town. He was not at all surprised to find Yussef the gold-smith running from one citizen to another and from one door to the next, to ask if anyone had seen his children.

'Oh Morad, Morad,' cried Yussef, wringing his hands distrac-tedly, 'can you not tell me where they are? In the name of Allah, come to my help!'

'Of course I will help you, friend Yussef, if I can,' said Morad. 'But what is wrong? What have you lost? Is it not written that one who will not help a friend in need is worse than a bucket with two holes in the bottom?'

'My children of course!' said Yussef frantically. 'I have lost my two dear children, my Bahram and my Soriyah. They have disappeared. They should have been home an hour ago. Have you seen anything of them?'

Morad paused, looked at the goldsmith and said very calmly:

'Perhaps I may be able to help. But I too am troubled, friend Yussef. I had the misfortune to lose my money-bag a few days ago. There were many gold and silver coins in it. I fancy that perhaps you know where it is. Did not the prophet say that —'

'Let us not talk of that now,' interrupted Yussef impatiently. 'What has become of my children? That is what really matters. Perhaps they have fallen down a well or strayed into the forest and been devoured by wolves.'

At this terrible thought, Yussef rolled his eyes in agony and clutched Morad's sleeve.

'No,' said the woodcarver, 'they have not fallen down a well or been eaten by wolves. They have been changed into little bears.'

'Changed into bears?' shouted Yussef in astonishment. 'That is ridiculous. You are making sport of me, Morad. Is this a time to mock me?'

'They are changed into bear-cubs,' repeated Morad quietly. 'I know, because I did it myself.'

'This is madness!' cried the goldsmith. 'How could you do such a thing?'

'That is my secret,' replied Morad. 'But be not anxious. When I get my money back, I will do my best to return your children. Until my money is restored, I am afraid your children will remain bear-cubs. Only my gold can give me the power to change them back into a little boy and girl. Ah well,' he continued with a sigh, 'they are very nice little bears. You will enjoy having them run about the house and climb trees for fruit. Did not the Book of Wisdom say, "Better a cheerful bear-cub than —"?'

'No, it did not!' broke in Yussef angrily. 'You are out of your mind. May all the plagues of the marsh and the desert light upon you, and may your sleep at night be tormented by djinns and foul spirits! I am going at once to the kalentar to tell him your crazy tale. You will be thrown into prison for this, you sorcerer, and possibly drowned in rancid oil.'

Waving his fists at Morad, the goldsmith ran off to the house of the kalentar. Now this was the chief magistrate, and his house stood by the courtroom of Allarcand. Here all the quarrels and disputes of the citizens were heard and judgement pronounced. If a man complained that a seller of pots and dishes had cheated him, if a woman believed that her neighbour had cast the evil eye upon her, if a father thought that his son was stealing his inheritance – all went to complain to the kalentar, and the kalentar dealt out justice before all the people.

Morad meanwhile, well pleased with himself and with a smile on his round face, strolled home to see if all was well with the two children and the bear-cubs. He was humming a popular song of the time as he unlocked his door and went in. Everything was peace and silence, and he stopped singing as he realized that all were asleep. He went into the kitchen to prepare his supper.

In the morning two fierce-looking officers with huge moustaches and long, curved swords, came to Morad's door to tell him that the kalentar wished to see him in the courthouse.

'Certainly,' agreed Morad. 'Can you tell me what is the reason for this summons?'

The chief officer told the woodcarver that there had been a complaint against him by Yussef the goldsmith – something about bewitching his children. Morad was to appear in half an hour.

When the officers had departed, twirling their swords and mustachios, Morad gave the two children breakfast in their little room upstairs. He told them he would soon send them home to their mother and father. Bahram and Soriyah had slept well and did not in the least mind staying with the woodcarver. He was their friend and he was kind to them. It was an amusing adventure to be away from home for once. They were almost sorry to hear they were soon to go back.

As for Lal and Kara, Morad gave them no breakfast. They were hungry and begged him piteously for food, running back and forth between Morad and the image of the goldsmith. When they found in his pockets no ripe peaches, no honey-cake, not so much as a dry biscuit, they cried, but Morad said:

'No breakfast today, my dears. Soon you will have to come into court, and then you must be hungry. Don't cry, little ones. It will not be for long.'

Next he went to a nearby house where lived a boy named Rustam, who sometimes helped him in his workshop. He was full of mischief and inclined to be idle. But when he wanted to earn a little money for sherbet or a new top to spin in the street, he would help Morad by sweeping up the shop or stacking a new load of timber. Just now it was for something quite different that Morad needed the boy's help.

Rustam already knew Lal and Kara. He had played with them, and the three were friends. They trusted him, and he had given them nuts. But now Morad forbade him to give them anything to eat. Instead, he made a loose knot in either end of a piece of rope and slipped it over their heads. He told Rustam to hold the rope in the middle.

'Now listen carefully,' he said. 'I'm going to the courthouse in the market place. Wait here, and in half an hour you are to follow after me and bring the cubs. Wait outside the courthouse until you are told to come in.'

Rustam nodded his head vigorously, and Morad left him and set off.

When they reached the courthouse, a crowd had already gathered to see what would happen. Rumours of an unusual case had reached them. There were always plenty of idlers in Allarcand, anxious to see what was to be seen and hear what was to be heard. There were carpenters, bricklayers, apprentice boys, bearded old men and housewives, a lame beggar hopping about on one leg and a ballad-singer trying to earn a few small coins from the impatient crowd. But few had ears for him. All were awaiting the arrival of Morad.

Inside the courthouse Yussef was already in his place, standing at one side with some of his friends. Morad, without greeting the goldsmith, took his stand at the other side.

The bell was rung, and for a moment there was silence. Through a door at the back of the courtroom came two officials and the kalentar or chief magistrate. He was very fat and very slow. He wore baggy velvet trousers, a purple waistcoat and a jewelled turban. In the centre of the platform was a carpet, and in the centre of the carpet was a high-backed chair. At one side of the carpet one of the officials squatted, ready to take notes. The other arranged the kalentar's hubble-bubble on a little carved table before him. The kalentar always smoked in court, but no one else was allowed to. Only he could breathe in the sweet smoke of forgetfulness while he heard the case.

The talking among the crowd had broken out again, and the kalentar held up his hand for silence. The official with the court papers muttered in the kalentar's ear while he lit his pipe. At last he sent out a cloud of rich smoke, and this was the signal that he was about to begin the hearing.

'Yussef the goldsmith,' he said slowly, 'you have a complaint against Morad the woodcarver. Stand forth, both of you.'

They obeyed, one on either side of the courtroom. Yussef was bursting with anger. He smoothed down his beard and cleared his throat.

'High and Mighty,' he said, 'the blessing of Allah upon you for a just judge! I accuse this rascal Morad of having stolen my two chief blessings, my son Bahram and my daughter Soriyah. Oh sir, if only you could see them. They are as the two chief jewels in the crown of his imperial majesty, the prince of all Persia —'

'Yes, yes,' interrupted the kalentar, pulling at his hubble-bubble, 'never mind about that. Go on.'

'This ruffian, as I say, sir,' Yussef went on, 'has stolen my children and hidden them away. I beg you to order him to give them back to me.'

'What do you say to this, Morad?' inquired the kalentar, turning ever so slightly in the direction of the woodcarver.

'It is perfectly true, O just judge,' Morad said calmly, a smile of self-satisfaction on his honest face. 'It is exactly as he says. Yussef the goldsmith, my false friend, stole my money-bag before I was awake. So I stole his children.'

At these words there were gasps of astonishment and a mur-muring in the court. People said:

'Morad is a kidnapper. Let him give back the children.'

But Morad's friends said:

'Yussef is a thief. Let him give back the money.'

'Morad,' said the kalentar, slowly and distinctly, 'if you have stolen the goldsmith's children – and it appears that you admit to doing so – is it not right that you should restore them? It is rather a serious matter to steal a man's children. In the book of laws, chapter – er – well, it is no matter which chapter, it distinctly says that it is a crime for one man to possess himself of the issue of another – or words to the same effect. What do you say?'

'High and Mighty,' said Morad, 'if the goldsmith restores my gold and silver, I will give him back his children.'

'What say you to that, Yussef?' drawled the fat kalentar, sending out another cloud of billowy, purple smoke.

'I can't give him his money,' answered Yussef, 'for I have not

got it. I did not take it. He is a liar, O just judge, as well as a
stealer of children. I demand the law of him!'

The kalentar sighed, for he was already feeling very tired.

'You are not here to demand anything, goldsmith,' he said
quietly, but his words were drowned by a roar from Yussef's
friends.

'Liar and kidnapper!' they shouted. 'Give him back his children, Morad. Give him back his children! Are not children more
than silver and gold?'

The kalentar banged on the table, and a court official rang a
bell. The kalentar shouted at the top of his voice, which was not
very loud:

'Silence in the court! Silence, I say.'

When the noise had died down, he continued:

'Do you hear what they are saying, Morad? They are saying
"Give him back his children". If you do not, things will go ill
with you.'

'To hear is to obey, O mighty judge,' Morad answered. 'But
unfortunately I cannot, for I have changed them into bear-cubs.
I will gladly give him the cubs, if he wants them.'

At this there was a tremendous sensation in the court. The
people could not believe their ears. They looked at Morad as if
he was an evil enchanter. A great babbling broke out, and once
more the kalentar called for order. He blew out an enormous
cloud of smoke, through which he said:

'If there is any more noise like that, I shall send for the guard
and clear the court. Morad, this is the most extraordinary thing I
have ever heard in the course of a hitherto uneventful life. I find
it hard to believe. Woodcarver, you will have to prove what you
have just said. By Allah, you will! Where are these so-called
bear-cubs, I should like to know? Can they be produced in
court?'

There was dead silence. Morad did not answer the kalentar,
but called to the boy Rustam, who was by now waiting outside:

'Rustam, bring in the bears, Bahram and Soriyah!'

There was general astonishment as Rustam led in the two cubs with the rope about their necks and stood at the end of the courtroom, facing the kalentar.

'Take the rope from their necks,' ordered Morad quietly.

Rustam did as he was told, and Morad went on:

'Have no fear, judge and people. They will do you no harm. They are only little children.'

For a few moments Lal and Kara stood side by side, blinking at all the people. They had never in their lives seen so many. Morad said:

'Go to your father, dear children. Perhaps he has food for you.'

The cubs' sharp eyes had already made out Yussef the goldsmith in his grey gown, pulling at his beard. Without hesitation they trotted up to him and began begging for food, rubbing their empty stomachs with their little paws most piteously. Yussef was too amazed to move. One of the cubs began licking his hands. The other knelt on the floor and put its arms round his knees, nuzzling its nose deep into his pockets. As the goldsmith bent down to push the cub away, the other licked him all over the face and beard. In the courtroom there was a sensation. Everyone was astonished at the novelty of this happening. Some laughed, others clapped their hands with delight, while people from outside, who had already heard rumours of this astonishing case, crowded in to the courtroom. Morad shouted triumphantly:

'There you are, O wise judge! See how the children know their father and how pleased they are to see him again. You ordered me to restore his children. I have done so in the sight of all these people. Now let him take them home and give me back my gold and silver.'

The crowd in the courtroom were puzzled. While some simply laughed with delight, others disputed about the matter; some said Morad really was an enchanter and had turned the children into bears, while others said they did not believe in miracles and that it must be a trick. As for Lal and Kara, now hungry as well as greedy, they were bitterly disappointed that the goldsmith had nothing for them to eat, but they still hoped he might feed them, as his image had fed them in the woodcarver's shop. They clung more tightly than ever round his waist, licking his hands, his face and his beard.

Everyone was laughing and cheering, and some cried:

'Take your children home, Yussef! Look after them better, or next time they may be turned into monkeys!'

In his embarrassment and distress, Yussef appealed to the kalentar:

'O mighty judge, protector of all the children of Allah, order this evil sorcerer to change these bears back to my beloved son and daughter.'

'Can you perform this feat, Morad?' inquired the kalentar sternly.

'I can try,' Morad replied. 'But I shall not suceeed while I am anxious about my money. If the goldsmith can find my money for me, perhaps I may be able to find his children. I know Bahram and Soriyah well in their human form. It would be a pity never to see such dear things again. Charming as are these bear-cubs —'

At this Yussef, in his desperation, broke down.

'O judge, be merciful to me,' he interrupted. 'What this man says is true. I am a wicked sinner and a thief. The Evil One entered my heart, and I stole the woodcarver's money. I don't know how I came to do it. There it lay under the fig tree. I was alone and I put it in my pocket. I will go and get it now, if only he will give me back my little girl and boy.'

'What do you say to this, Morad?' asked the kalentar with a weary sigh. It had been a very trying case, and a very noisy one.

'I agree,' said Morad promptly. 'Let him return here with my money, and I will take away the bear-cubs and change them once more into children.'

'Very well,' said the kalentar. 'Let it be done.'

As Yussef hurried away, Morad led the bear-cubs out of the courtroom, and the fat kalentar dropped off into a well-earned sleep.

So ends the story of the thieving goldsmith and the clever woodcarver. In half an hour both were back in court. The attendants woke up the kalentar, and the people stopped playing dice and peeling oranges. Yussef handed over the leather money-bag. Morad came in with little Bahram and Soriyah, each holding one of his hands. Before letting Yussef have them he counted over the gold and silver pieces to make sure they were all there. For is it not written that he who would thrive in business must trust no one, not even his own flesh and blood?

The kalentar ordered Yussef and Morad to embrace and make friends, and this they did. Yussef was overjoyed to get his son and daughter back. No harm had come to them, and they told him how kind the woodcarver had been. Together they left the courtroom amidst general satisfaction and applause.

When Morad got back to his house, he found Rustam there with the bear-cubs. They had all grown fond of each other. They had a feast of spiced cakes and crystallized fruits from the cupboard. Then Morad told the boy to take the cubs away into the forest and give them their freedom. They lost no time in scampering away to climb trees for nuts and apples. If Lal could have spoken, as perhaps in bear-language he could, he would have said:

'Is it not written, my sister, that the wild apples from one's own forest are better than the honey-cakes from a stranger's cupboard?'

Arap Sang and the Cranes

an African tale
retold by Humphrey Harman

The people of Africa believe that before you give anything to anyone you should first carefully think out what your gift will mean to him. They are often shocked at the way white men give things, anything, tractors, and trousers, guns and radios, showering them down on people's heads with no kind of thought about what they will *mean* to the people who get the presents. Like being given a camera when you can't afford to buy films. That's worse than not having a camera.

A gift is a great responsibility to the giver, they say, and after they have said that they may tell you the story of Arap Sang and the Cranes.

Arap Sang was a great chief and more than half a god, for in the days when he lived great chiefs were always a little mixed up with the gods. One day he was walking on the plain admiring the cattle.

It was hot. The rains had not yet come; the ground was almost bare of grass and as hard as stone; the thorn trees gave no shade, for they were just made of long spines and thin twigs and tiny leaves, and the sun went straight through them.

It was hot. Only the black ants didn't feel it and they would be happy in a furnace.

Arap Sang was getting old and the sun beat down on his bald head (he was sensitive about this and didn't like it mentioned) and he thought: 'I'm feeling things more than I used.'

And then he came across a vulture sitting in the crotch of a tree, his wings hanging down and his eyes on the look-out.

'Vulture,' said Arap Sang, 'I'm hot and the sun is making my head ache. You have there a fine pair of broad wings. I'd be most grateful if you'd spread them out and let an old man enjoy a patch of shade.'

'Why?' croaked Vulture. He had indigestion. Vultures usually have indigestion, it's the things they eat.

'Why?' said Arap Sang mildly. 'Now that's a question to which I'm not certain that I've got the answer. Why? Why, I suppose, because I ask you. Because I'm an old man and entitled to a little assistance and respect. Because it wouldn't be much trouble to you. Because it's pleasant and good to help people.'

'Bah!' said Vulture.

'What's that?'

'Oh, go home, Baldy, and stop bothering people, it's hot.'

Arap Sang straightened himself up and his eyes flashed. He wasn't half a god for nothing and when he was angry he could be rather a terrible old person. And he was very angry now. It was that remark about his lack of hair.

The really terrifying thing was that when he spoke he didn't shout. He spoke quietly and the words were clear and cold and hard. And all separate like hailstones.

'Vulture,' he said, 'you're cruel and you're selfish. I shan't forget what you've said and you won't either. NOW GET OUT!'

Arap Sang was so impressive that Vulture got up awkwardly and flapped off.

'Silly old fool,' he said, uncomfortably.

Presently he met an acquaintance of his (vultures don't have friends, they just have acquaintances) and they perched together on the same bough. Vulture took a close look at his companion and then another and what he saw was so funny that it cheered him up.

'He, he!' he giggled. 'What's happened to you? Met with an accident? You're bald.'

The other vulture looked sour, but at the same time you felt he might be pleased about something.

'That's good, coming from you,' he said. 'What have you been

up to? You haven't got a feather on you above the shoulders.'

Then they both felt their heads with consternation. It was quite true. They were bald, both of them, and so was every other vulture, the whole family, right down to this very day.

Which goes to show that if you can't be ordinarily pleasant to people at least it's not wise to go insulting great chiefs who are half gods.

I said that he was rather a terrible old person.

Arap Sang walked on. He was feeling shaky. Losing his temper always upset him afterwards and doing the sort of magic that makes every vulture in the world bald in the wink of an eye, takes it out of you if you aren't as young as you used to be.

And he did want a bit of shade.

Presently he met an elephant. Elephant was panting across the plain in a tearing hurry and was most reluctant to stop when Arap Sang called to him.

'Elephant,' said Arap Sang weakly, 'I'm tired and I'm dizzy. I want to get to the forest and into a bit of shade but it's a long way.'

'It is hot, isn't it?' said Elephant. 'I'm off to the forest myself.'

'Would you spread out your great ears and let me walk along under them?' asked Arap Sang.

'I'm sorry,' said Elephant, 'but you'd make my journey so slow. I must get to the forest. I've got the most terrible headache.'

'Well, I've got a headache too,' protested the old man.

'I'm sure you have,' said Elephant, 'and no one could be sorrier about that than I am. Is it a very big headache?'

'Shocking big,' said Arap Sang.

'There now,' said Elephant. 'Consider how big I am compared to you and what the size of my headache must be.'

That's elephants all over, always so logical. Arap Sang felt that there was something wrong with this argument but he couldn't just see where. Also he had become a little uncomfortable about all those bald vultures and he didn't want to lose his temper with anyone else. You have to be careful what you do when you're half a god. It's so dreadfully final.

'Oh, all right,' he muttered.

'Knew you'd see it that way,' said Elephant. 'It's just what I was saying about you the other day. You can always rely on Arap Sang, I said, to behave reasonably. Well, good-bye and good luck.'

And he hurried off in the direction of the distant forest and was soon out of sight.

Poor Arap Sang was now feeling very ill indeed. He sat on the ground and he thought to himself: 'I can't go another step unless I get some shade and if I don't get some soon I'm done for.'

And there he was found by a flock of cranes.

They came dancing through the white grass, stamping their long delicate legs so that the insects flew up in alarm and were at once snapped up in the cranes' beaks. They gathered round Arap Sang sitting on the ground, and he looked so old and distressed that they hopped up and down with embarrassment, first on one leg then the other. 'Korong! Korong!' they called softly and this happens to be their name as well.

'Good birds,' whispered Arap Sang, 'you must help me. If I don't reach shade soon I'll die. Help me to the forest.'

'But of course,' said the cranes, and they spread their great handsome black and white wings to shade him and helped him to his feet, and together, slowly, they all crossed the plain into the trees.

Then Arap Sang sat in the shade of a fine cotton tree and felt very much better. The birds gathered round him and he looked at them and thought that he had never seen more beautiful creatures in the whole world.

'And kind. Kind as well as beautiful,' he muttered. 'The two don't always go together. I must reward them.'

'I shan't forget your kindness,' he said, 'and I'll see that no one else does. Now I want each one of you to come here.'

Then the cranes came one after another and bowed before him and Arap Sang stretched out his kindly old hand and gently touched each beautiful sleek head. And where he did this a golden crown appeared and after the birds had gravely bowed

their thanks they all flew off to the lake, their new crowns glittering in the evening sun.

Arap Sang felt quite recovered. He was very pleased with his gift to the cranes.

Two months later a crane dragged himself to the door of Arap Sang's house. It was a pitiful sight, thin with hunger, feathers broken and muddy from hiding in the reeds, eyes red with lack of sleep.

Arap Sang exclaimed in pity and horror.

'Great Chief,' said the crane, 'we beg you to take back your gift. If you don't there'll soon be not one crane left alive, for we are hunted day and night for the sake of our golden crowns.'

Arap Sang listened and nodded his head in sorrow.

'I'm old and I'm foolish,' he said, 'and I harm my friends. I had forgotten that men also were greedy and selfish and that they'll do anything for gold. Let me undo the wrong I have done by giving without thought. I'll make one more magic but that'll be the last.'

Then he took their golden crowns and in their place he put a wonderful halo of feathers which they have until this day.

But they are still called Crowned Cranes.

Belinda and Bellamant

by E. Nesbit

There is a certain country where a king is never allowed to reign
while a queen can be found. They like queens much better than
kings in that country. I can't think why. If someone has tried to
teach you a little history, you will perhaps think that this is the
Salic Law. But it isn't. In the biggest city of that odd country
there is a great bell-tower (higher than the clock-tower of the
Houses of Parliament, where they put MPs who forget their
manners). This bell-tower had seven bells in it, very sweet-
toned splendid bells, made expressly to ring on the joyful
occasions when a princess was born who would be queen some
day. And the great tower was built expressly for the bells to ring
in. So you see what a lot they thought of queens in that country.
Now in all the bells there are Bell-people – it is their voices that
you hear when the bells ring. All that about its being the clapper
of the bell is mere nonsense, and would hardly deceive a child. I
don't know why people say such things. Most Bell-people are
very energetic and busy. They love the sound of their own
voices, and hate being idle, and when nearly two hundred years
had gone by, and no princesses had been born, they got tired of
living in bells that were never rung. So they slipped out of the
belfry one fine frosty night, and left the big beautiful bells
empty, and went off to find other homes. One of them went to
live in a dinner-bell, and one in a school-bell, and the rest all
found homes – they did not mind where – just anywhere, in
fact, where they could find any Bell-person kind enough to give
them board and lodging. And everyone was surprised at the
increased loudness in the voices of these hospitable bells. For, of

course, the Bell-people from the belfry did their best to help in the housework as polite guests should, and always added their voices to those of their hosts on all occasions when bell-talk was called for. And the seven big beautiful bells in the belfry were left hollow and dark and quite empty, except for the clappers who did not care about the comforts of a home.

Now of course a good house does not remain empty long, especially when there is no rent to pay, and in a very short time the seven bells all had tenants, and they were all the kind of folk that no respectable Bell-people would care to be acquainted with.

They had been turned out of other bells – cracked bells and broken bells, the bells of horses that had been lost in snowstorms or of ships that had gone down at sea. They hated work, and they were a glum, silent, disagreeable people, but as far as they could be pleased about anything they were pleased to live in bells that were never rung, in houses where there was nothing to do. They sat hunched up under the black domes of their houses, dressed in darkness and cobwebs, and their only pleasure was idleness, their only feasts the thick dusty silence that lies heavy in all belfries where the bells never ring. They hardly ever spoke even to each other, and then it was in the whispers that Bell-people talk in among themselves; and that no one can hear but the bat whose ear for music is very fine and who has himself a particularly high voice; and when they did speak they quarrelled.

And when at last the bells were rung for the birth of a princess the wicked Bell-people were furious. Of course they had to ring – a bell can't help that when the rope is pulled – but their voices were so ugly that people were quite shocked.

'What poor taste our ancestors must have had,' they said, 'to think these were good bells!'

(You remember the bells had not rung for nearly two hundred years.)

'Dear me,' said the king to the queen, 'what odd ideas people had in the old days, I always understood that these bells had beautiful voices.'

'They're quite hideous,' said the queen. And so they were. Now that night the lazy Bell-folk came down out of the belfry full of anger against the princess whose birth had disturbed their idleness. There is no anger like that of a lazy person who is made to work against his will.

And they crept out of the dark domes of their houses and came down in their dust dresses and cobweb cloaks, and crept up to the palace where everyone had gone to bed long before, and stood round the mother-of-pearl cradle where the baby princess lay asleep. And they reached their seven dark right hands out across the white satin coverlet, and the oldest and hoarsest and laziest said:

'She shall grow uglier every day, except Sundays, and every Sunday she shall be seven times prettier than the Sunday before.'

'Why not uglier every day, and a double dose on Sunday?' asked the youngest and spitefullest of the wicked Bell-people.

'Because there's no rule without an exception,' said the eldest and hoarsest and laziest, 'and she'll feel it all the more if she's pretty once a week. And,' he added, 'this shall go on till she finds a bell that doesn't ring, and can't ring, and never will ring, and wasn't made to ring.'

'Why not for ever?' asked the young and spiteful.

'Nothing goes on for ever,' said the eldest Bell-person, 'not even ill-luck. And we have to leave her a way out. It doesn't matter. She'll never know what it is. Let alone finding it.'

Then they went back to the belfry and rearranged as well as they could the comfortable web-and-owls'-nest furniture of their houses which had all been shaken up and disarranged by that absurd ringing of bells at the birth of a princess that nobody could really be pleased about.

When the princess was two weeks old the king said to the queen:

'My love – the princess is not so handsome as I thought she was.'

'Nonsense, Henry,' said the queen, 'the light's not good, that's all.'

Next day – it was Sunday – the king pulled back the lace curtains of the cradle and said:

'The light's good enough now – and you see she's –'

He stopped.

'It must have been the light,' he said, 'she looks all right to-day.'

'Of course she does, a precious,' said the queen.

But on Monday morning His Majesty was quite sure really that the princess was rather plain, for a princess. And when Sunday came, and the princess had on her best robe and the cap with the little white ribbons in the frill, he rubbed his nose and said there was no doubt dress did make a great deal of difference. For the princess was now as pretty as a new daisy.

The princess was several years old before her mother could be got to see that it really was better for the child to wear plain clothes and a veil on week-days. On Sundays, of course, she could wear her best frock and a clean crown just like anybody else.

Of course nobody ever told the princess how ugly she was.

She wore a veil on week-days, and so did everyone else in the palace, and she was never allowed to look in the glass except on Sundays, so that she had no idea that she was not as pretty all the week as she was on the first day of it. She grew up therefore quite contented. But the parents were in despair.

'Because,' said King Henry, 'it's high time she was married. We ought to choose a king to rule the realm – I have always looked forward to her marrying at twenty-one – and to our retiring on a modest competence to some nice little place in the country where we could have a few pigs.'

'And a cow,' said the queen, wiping her eyes.

'And a pony and trap,' said the king.

'And hens,' said the queen, 'yes. And now it can never, never be. Look at the child! I just ask you! Look at her!'

'No,' said the king firmly, 'I haven't done that since she was ten, except on Sundays.'

'Couldn't we get a prince to agree to a "Sundays only" marriage – not let him see her during the week?'

'Such an unusual arrangement,' said the king, 'would involve very awkward explanations, and I can't think of any except the true ones, which would be quite impossible to give. You see, we should want a first-class prince, and no really high-toned Highness would take a wife on those terms.'

'It's a thoroughly comfortable kingdom,' said the queen doubtfully. 'The young man would be handsomely provided for for life.'

'I couldn't marry Belinda to a time-server or a place-worshipper,' said the king decidely.

Meanwhile the princess had taken the matter into her own hands. She had fallen in love.

You know, of course, that a handsome book is sent out every year to all the kings who have daughters to marry. It is rather like the illustrated catalogues of Liberty's or Peter Robinson's, only instead of illustrations showing furniture or ladies' cloaks and dresses, the pictures are all of princes who are of an age to be married, and are looking out for suitable wives. The book is called *The Royal Match Catalogue Illustrated* – and besides the pictures of the princes it has little printed bits about their incomes, accomplishments, prospects, tempers and relations.

Now the princess saw this book – which is never shown to princesses, but only to their parents – when it was carelessly left lying on the round table in the parlour. She looked all through it, and she hated each prince more than the one before till she came to the very end, and on the last page of all, screwed away in a corner, was the picture of a prince who was quite as good-looking as a prince has any call to be.

'I like you,' said Belinda softly. Then she read the little bit of print underneath.

Prince Bellamant, aged twenty-four. Wants princess who doesn't object to a christening curse. Nature of curse only revealed in the strictest of confidence. Good-tempered. Comfortably off. Quiet habits. No relations.

'Poor dear,' said the princess. 'I wonder what the curse is! I'm sure I shouldn't mind!'

The blue dusk of evening was deepening in the garden outside. The princess rang for the lamp and went to draw the curtain. There was a rustle and a faint high squeak – and something black flopped fluttering on to the floor.

'Oh – it's a bat,' cried the princess, as the lamp came in. 'I don't like bats.

'Let me fetch a dust-pan and brush and sweep the nasty thing away,' said the parlour-maid.

'No, no,' said Belinda, 'it's hurt, poor dear,' and though she hated bats she picked it up. It was horribly cold to touch, and one wing dragged loosely. 'You can go, Jane,' said the princess to the parlour-maid.

Then she got a big velvet-covered box that had had chocolate in it, and put some cotton wool in it and said to the bat –

'You poor dear, is that comfortable?' and the bat said:

'Quite, thanks.'

'Good gracious,' said the princess, jumping. 'I didn't know bats could talk.'

'Everyone can talk,' said the bat, 'but not everyone can hear other people talking. You have a fine ear as well as a fine heart.'

'Will your wing ever get well?' asked the princess.

'I hope so,' said the bat. 'But let's talk about you. Do you know why you wear a veil every day except Sundays?'

'Doesn't everybody?' asked Belinda.

'Only here in the palace,' said the bat. 'That's on your account.'

'But why?' asked the princess.

'Look in the glass and you'll know.'

'But it's wicked to look in the glass except on Sundays – and besides they're all put away,' said the princess.

'If I were you,' said the bat, 'I should go up into the attic where the youngest kitchen-maid sleeps. Feel between the thatch and the wall just above her pillow, and you'll find a little round looking-glass. But come back here before you look at it.'

The princess did exactly what the bat told her to do, and when she had come back into the parlour and shut the door she looked in the little round glass that the youngest kitchen-maid's sweetheart had given her. And when she saw her ugly, ugly, ugly face – for you must remember she had been growing uglier every day since she was born – she screamed and then she said:

'That's not me, it's a horrid picture.'

'It is you, though,' said the bat firmly but kindly; 'and now you see why you wear a veil all the week – and only look in the glass on Sunday.'

'But why,' asked the princess in tears, 'why don't I look like that in the Sunday looking-glasses?'

'Because you aren't like that on Sundays,' the bat replied. 'Come,' it went on, 'stop crying. I didn't tell you the dread secret of your ugliness just to make you cry – but because I know the way for you to be as pretty all the week as you are on Sundays, and since you've been kind to me I'll tell you. Sit down.'

The princess did, and listened through her veil and her tears, while the bat told her all that I began this story by telling you.

'My great-great-great-great-grandfather heard the tale years ago,' he said, 'up in the dark, dusty, beautiful, comfortable, cobwebby belfry, and I have heard scraps of it myself when the evil Bell-people were quarrelling, or talking in their sleep, lazy things!'

'It's very good of you to tell me all this,' said Belinda, 'but what am I to do?'

'You must find the bell that doesn't ring, and can't ring, and never will ring, and wasn't made to ring.'

'If I were a prince,' said the princess, 'I could go out and seek my fortune.'

'Princesses have fortunes as well as princes,' said the bat.

'But Father and Mother would never let me go and look for mine.'

'Think!' said the bat. 'Perhaps you'll find a way.'

So Belinda thought and thought. And at last she got the book that had the portraits of eligible princes in it, and she wrote to the prince who had the christening curse – and this is what she said:

'Princess Belinda of Carillon-land is not afraid of christening curses. If Prince Bellamant would like to marry her he had better apply to her Royal Father in the usual way.

'P.S. – I have seen your portrait.'

When the prince got this letter he was very pleased, and wrote at once for Princess Belinda's likeness. Of course they sent him a picture of her Sunday face, which was the most beautiful face in the world. As soon as he saw it he knew that this was not only the most beautiful face in the world, but the dearest, so he wrote to her father by the next post – applying for her hand in the usual way and enclosing the most respectable references. The king told the princess.

'Come,' said he, 'what do you say to this young man?'

And the princess, of course, said, 'Yes, please.'

So the wedding-day was fixed for the first Sunday in June.

But when the prince arrived with all his glorious following of courtiers and men-at-arms, with two pink peacocks and a crown-case full of diamonds for his bride, he absolutely refused to be married on a Sunday. Nor would he give any reason for his refusal. And then the king lost his temper and broke off the match, and the prince went away.

But he did not go very far. That night he bribed a page-boy to show him which was the princess's room, and he climbed up by the jasmine through the dark rose-scented night, and he tapped at the window.

'Who's dhere?' said the princess inside in the dark.

'Me,' said the prince in the dark outside.

'Thed id wasnd't true?' said the princess. 'They toad be you'd ridded away.'

'What a cold you've got, my princess,' said the prince, hanging on by the jasmine boughs.

'It's not a cold,' sniffed the princess.

'Then . . . oh, you dear . . . were you crying because you thought I'd gone?' he said.

'I suppose so,' said she.

He said, 'You dear!' again, and kissed her hands.

'Why wouldn't you be married on a Sunday?' she asked.

'It's the curse, dearest,' he explained, 'I couldn't tell anyone but you. The fact is Malevola wasn't asked to my christening so she doomed me to be . . . well, she said "moderately good-looking all the week, and too ugly for words on Sundays". So you see! You will be married on a week-day, won't you?'

'But I can't,' said the princess, 'because I've got a curse too – only I'm ugly all the week and pretty on Sundays.'

'How extremely tiresome,' said the prince, 'but can't you be cured?'

'Oh yes,' said the princess, and told him how. 'And you,' she asked, 'is yours quite incurable?'

'Not at all,' he answered, 'I've only got to stay under water for five minutes and the spell will be broken. But you see, beloved, the difficulty is that I can't do it. I've practised regularly, from a boy, in the sea, and in the swimming bath, and even in my wash-hand basin – hours at a time I've practised – but I never can keep under more than two minutes.

'Oh dear,' said the princess, 'this is dreadful.'

'It is rather trying,' the prince answered.

'You're sure you like me,' she asked suddenly, 'now you know that I'm only pretty once a week?'

'I'd die for you,' said he.

'Then I'll tell you what. Send all your courtiers away, and take a situation as under-gardener here – I know we want one. And then every night I'll climb down the jasmine and we'll go out together and seek our fortune. I'm sure we shall find it.'

And they did go out. The very next night, and the next, and the next, and the next, and the next, and the next. And they did not find their fortunes, but they got fonder and fonder of each other. They could not see each other's faces, but they held hands as they went along through the dark.

And on the seventh night, as they passed by a house that showed chinks of light through its shutters, they heard a bell being rung outside for supper, a bell with a very loud and beautiful voice. But instead of saying –

'Supper's ready,' as anyone would have expected, the bell was saying –

> 'Ding dong dell!
> I could tell
> Where you ought to go
> To break the spell.'

Then someone left off ringing the bell, so of course it couldn't say any more. So the two went on. A little way down the road a cow-bell tinkled behind the wet hedge of the lane. And it said – not, 'Here I am, quite safe,' as a cow-bell should, but –

> 'Ding dong dell
> All will be well
> If you . . .'

Then the cow stopped walking and began to eat, so the bell couldn't say any more. The prince and princess went on, and you will not be surprised to hear that they heard the voices of five more bells that night. The next was a school-bell. The schoolmaster's little boy thought it would be fun to ring it very late at night – but his father came and caught him before the bell could say any more than –

> 'Ding dong dell
> You can break up the spell
> By taking . . .'

So that was no good.

Then there were the three bells that were the sign over the door of an inn where people were happily dancing to a fiddle, because there was a wedding. These bells said:

> 'We are the
> Merry three
> Bells, bells, bells.
> You are two
> To undo
> Spells, spells, spells . . .'

Then the wind who was swinging the bells suddenly thought of an appointment he had made with a pine forest to get up an entertaining imitation of sea-waves for the benefit of the forest nymphs who had never been to the seaside, and he went off – so, of course, the bells couldn't ring any more, and the prince and princess went on down the dark road.

There was a cottage and the princess pulled her veil closely over her face, for yellow light streamed from its open door – and it was a Wednesday.

Inside a little boy was sitting on the floor – quite a little boy – he ought to have been in bed long before, and I don't know why he wasn't. And he was ringing a little tinkling bell that had dropped off a sleigh.

And this little bell said:

> 'Tinkle, tinkle, tinkle, I'm a little sleigh-bell,
> But I know what I know, and I'll tell, tell, tell.
> Find the Enchanter of the Ringing Well,

He will show you how to break the spell, spell, spell.
Tinkle, tinkle, I'm a little sleigh-bell,
But I know what I know . . .'
And so on, over and over, again and again, because the little
boy was quite contented to go on shaking his sleigh-bell for ever
and ever.

'So now we know,' said the prince, 'isn't that glorious?'

'Yes, very, but where's the Enchanter of the Ringing Well?'
said the princess doubtfully.

'Oh, I've got his address in my pocket-book,' said the prince.
'He's my god-father. He was one of the references I gave to your
father.'

So the next night the prince brought a horse to the garden,
and he and the princess mounted, and rode, and rode, and
rode, and in the grey dawn they came to Wonderwood, and in
the very middle of that the Enchanter's Palace stands.

The princess did not like to call on a perfect stranger so very
early in the morning, so they decided to wait a little and look
about them.

The castle was very beautiful, decorated with a conventional design of bells and bell-ropes, carved in stone.

Luxuriant plants of American bell-vine covered the draw-bridge and portcullis. On a green lawn in front of the castle was a well, with a curious bell-shaped covering suspended over it. The lovers leaned over the mossy fern-grown wall of the well, and, looking down, they could see that the narrowness of the well only lasted for a few feet, and below that it spread into a cavern where water lay in a big pool.

'What cheer?' said a pleasant voice behind them. It was the Enchanter, an early riser, like Darwin was, and all other great scientific men.

They told him what cheer.

'But,' Prince Bellamant ended, 'it's really no use. I can't keep under water more than two minutes however much I try. And my precious Belinda's not likely to find any silly old bell that doesn't ring, and can't ring, and never will ring, and was never made to ring.'

'Ho, ho,' laughed the Enchanter with the soft full laughter of old age. 'You've come to the right shop. Who told you?'

'The bells,' said Belinda.

'Ah yes,' The old man frowned kindly upon them. 'You must be very fond of each other?'

'We are,' said the two together.

'Yes,' the Enchanter answered, 'because only true lovers can hear the true speech of the bells, and then only when they're together. Well, there's the bell!'

He pointed to the covering of the well, went forward, and touched some lever or spring. The covering swung out from above the well, and hung over the grass grey with the dew of dawn.

'That?' said Bellamant.

'That,' said his god-father, 'is what's called a diving bell. It doesn't ring, and it can't ring, and it never will ring, and it was never made to ring. Get into it.'

'Eh?' said Bellamant, forgetting his manners.

The old man took a hand of each and led them under the bell.

They looked up. It had windows of thick glass, and high seats about four feet from its edge, running all round inside.

'Take your seats,' said the Enchanter.

Bellamant lifted his princess to the bench and leaped up beside her.

'Now,' said the old man, 'sit still, hold each other's hands, and for your lives don't move.'

He went away, and the next moment they felt the bell swing in the air. It swung round till once more it was over the well, and then it went down, down, down.

'I'm not afraid, with you,' said Belinda, because she was, dreadfully.

Down went the bell. The glass windows leaped into light, and, looking through them , the two could see blurred glories of lamps in the side of the well. Then with a plop the lower edge of the bell met the water, the water rose inside, a little, then not any more. And the bell went down, down, and above their heads the green water lapped against the windows of the bell.

'You're under water – if we stay five minutes,' Belinda whispered.

'Yes, dear,' said Bellamant, and pulled out his ruby-studded chronometer.

'It's five minutes for you, but oh!' cried Belinda, 'it's now for me. For I've found the bell that doesn't ring, and can't ring, and never will ring, and wasn't made to ring. Oh Bellamant dearest, it's Thursday. Have I got my Sunday face?'

She tore away her veil, and his eyes, fixed upon her face, could not leave it.

'Oh dream of all the world's delight,' he murmured, 'how beautiful you are.'

Neither spoke again till a sudden little shock told them that the bell was moving up again.

'Nonsense,' said Bellamant, 'it's not five minutes.'

But when they looked at the ruby-studded chronometer, it was nearly three-quarters of an hour. But then, of course, the well was enchanted.

'Magic? Nonsense,' said the old man when they hung about

67

him with thanks and pretty words. 'As I told you, it's only a diving bell.'

So they went home and were married, and the princess did not wear a veil at the wedding. She said she had had enough veils to last her a life-time.

And a year and a day after that a little daughter was born to them.

'Now, sweetheart,' said King Bellamant – he was king now because the old king and queen had retired from the business, and were keeping pigs and hens in the country as they had always planned to do – 'I am going to ring the bells with my own hands, to show how glad I am for you, and for the child, and for our good life together.'

So he went out. It was very dark, because the baby princess had chosen to be born at midnight.

The king went out to the belfry, that stood in the great, bare, quiet, moonlit square, and he opened the door. The furry-pussy bell-ropes, like huge caterpillars, hung on the first loft. The king began to climb the curly-wurly stone stair. And as he went up he heard a noise, the strangest noises, stamping and rustling and deep breathings.

He stood still in the ringers' loft where the pussy-furry cater-pillary bell-ropes hung, and from the belfry above he heard the noise of strong fighting, and mixed with it the sound of voices angry and desperate, but with a noble note that thrilled the soul of the hearer like the sound of the trumpet in battle. And the voices cried:

> 'Down, down – away, away,
> When good has come ill may not stay,
> Out, out, into the night,
> The belfry bells are ours by right!'

And the words broke and joined again, like water when it flows against the piers of a bridge. 'Down, down –.' 'Ill may not stay –.' 'Good has come –.' 'Away, away –.' And the joining came like the sound of the river that flows free again.

'Out, out, into the night,
The belfry bells are ours by right!'
And then, as King Bellamant stood there, thrilled and yet, as
it were, turned to stone, by the magic of this conflict that raged
above him, there came a sweeping rush down the belfry ladder.
The lantern he carried showed him a rout of little, dark, evil
people, clotted in dust and cobwebs, that scurried down the
wooden steps gnashing their teeth and growling in the bitter-
ness of a deserved defeat. They passed and there was silence.
Then the king flew from rope to rope pulling lustily, and from
above the bells answered in their own clear beautiful voices –
because the good Bell-people had driven out the usurpers and
had come to their own again.

'Ring-a-ring-a-ring-a-ring-a-ring! Ring, bell!
A little baby comes on earth to dwell. Ring, bell!
Sound, bell! Sound! Swell!
Ring for joy and wish her well!
May her life tell
No tale of ill-spell!
Ring, bell! Joy, bell!
Ring!'

The Popplesnitch

a tale from Lithuania
retold by Agnes Szudek

Bartek was a first-class shot with a gun. His keen eye and steady aim had secured for him a good job with a rich landowner. He guarded the eastern side of the property against packs of wolves that often attacked his master's thoroughbred horses.

But something had gone wrong. During a particularly severe winter, the wolves were driven mad with hunger and managed to make off with several of the livestock, in spite of Bartek's diligence.

Since then, he had lost the knack of using his gun, and was in danger of losing his job too, and the cosy little cottage that went with it.

Bartek was ashamed and worried. He practised every day for hours, aiming at pots and boxes, but every time he fired – he missed.

'I give up!' he cried in despair. 'It looks like a beggar's life for me, from now on. Oh, what wouldn't I give to be a good shot again!'

As he spoke, a bush nearby parted in the middle, and out stepped a strange thin man in a big hat and a long coat.

'Good day, sir! Good day, good day, good day!' exclaimed the figure in a very friendly manner.

Bartek immediately pointed his gun at the man. 'Who are you?' he asked sternly. 'This is my master's land and trespassers are not allowed. What's your business here?'

In answer the man came closer to Bartek, quite unafraid of the gun that was still levelled at him.

'I'm a wayfarer, a simple traveller, a passer-by! Call me what you will, but I'm not a thief. I make a fair exchange for every-thing I take.'

Bartek lowered his gun and, as he scrutinized the stranger, he thought he saw a tail whisking about behind his coat, but within a second it flicked out of sight, and Bartek thought he must have imagined it.

'Well,' he said, 'if you're here on business, my master's house is straight along the path, you can't miss it.'

'It's you I want to see,' said the stranger with a sly twisted smile. 'I hear you're a bad shot, and you'd give much to improve.'

'Is that so? Then your ears are pretty sharp,' said Bartek indignantly. 'What business is it of yours?'

'Many things are my business,' smirked the stranger. 'I could make you an expert shot – for a small exchange. In fact I could make you the finest marksman in the country.'

'The finest – could you really?' gasped Bartek, with his eye lighting up. 'Oh well, in that case an exchange of any size would be worth while. I don't want to lose my job, do I? Go on, tell me what is it you want.'

The thin man folded his arms and looked very superior. 'I'm quite a reasonable fellow,' he said, 'so let's strike a neat bargain. As you probably know, a magic word here and there can work wonders. Now, with one of my rare words I can make you a perfect shot, and for a whole year you can enjoy your fame. At the end of the year, I will simply ask you to show me a rare bird, and if I cannot name it, the power will be yours for good. If, however, I am able to name the bird, then you must come with me as a slave, for ever. How does that sound?'

'Most reasonable!' cried Bartek happily. 'Oh you are a reason-able man indeed! I agree. At the end of the year – a rare bird. I promise I won't forget.'

'Never fear, I'll be back to remind you,' grinned the stranger. 'And now let me introduce myself. I am Rokita, the one and only!' As he said this he took off his hat and bowed low, and Bartek saw two horns sticking out of the top of his head.

The poor man opened and closed his mouth with shock,

before any words came out. '*Rokita*? The forest demon?' he
screeched. 'I knew it! I thought I saw a tail about you. Oh what
have I done!' Bartek staggered about holding his head in horror.

'You've made an agreement with me, which you cannot
break, that's all,' laughed Rokita. 'Remember, if you fail to keep
your word, the earth will open up and swallow you. I can easily
arrange it.'

Bartek's first thought was to shoot the demon and be rid of
him. Without thinking further, he raised his gun and fired at
point-blank range – but he missed!

The demon roared with laughter until the leaves quivered on
their branches and the roots of the trees groaned in the earth.
Rokita's laughter rumbled on like thunder while Bartek waited
dejectedly for it to stop.

'Think well on it, you have twelve months exactly to find a
rare bird,' said the demon at last. 'If you fail, you are mine for
ever.'

With his forked tail trailing behind him, he began to run
round in a circle, jabbering:

     'Take my rare word for your rare bird.

     Take my rare word for your rare bird.

A rare word for a rare bird.
A rare word for a rare bird.
Bird – word – bird – word . . .'

Faster and faster went Rokita until the words could no longer be understood, then he whizzed up into the air like a little cyclone and vanished from sight. In the place where he had been chanting his rhyme, there lay a brand-new shotgun. At first Bartek did not see it. He was too busy looking up at the sky.

'Now I've done it,' he moaned. 'How can I ever get the better of a demon, and what do I know about birds?' It was true he knew all the wildfowl of his marshy homeland, but he had never travelled more than a few miles away in any direction.

He was about to trudge off home when he saw the new gun lying on the grass. Kneeling down, he gazed at it in wonder. It was the most beautiful gun he had ever seen. The steel barrel glinted in the sunlight, and the butt was decorated with inlaid silver and mother-of-pearl. And it was inscribed with his own name – BARTEK.

'Oh blessed gift!' he cried. 'If my life depended on it, I couldn't resist this little gun.' He was so excited that he forgot about the demon who had given it to him. Lovingly he held the gun in his arms and carried it home.

From that day onwards, Bartek's life changed. His master did not lose another of his horses. Any wolf that came within sniffing range was as good as dead. Bartek was a perfect marksman and his skill was the talk of the district.

But the day came when he realized that the demon would soon return, and he had not so much as thought of finding a rare bird. Now that he was such a success, he felt less inclined to be taken into slavery by the demon. Bartek was a very worried man.

One morning in early summer he was sitting outside his cottage eating breakfast by the banks of the river when he heard someone calling him.

'Hi there! Have you seen my cow? She's black-and-white, dainty as a dandelion, and I can't find her.'

Bartek saw a woman coming towards him in a flat-bottomed

73

boat. Deftly she wielded the long pole until she had brought the boat alongside.

'Well,' she shouted. 'Have you seen her?'

'What, your cow? No,' replied Bartek, and he was instantly struck by the woman's astonishing ugliness. He had never seen anyone quite so ugly before. Her nose was big, her ears were bigger, her mouth was crooked and her eyes were small. He took all this in at a glance.

'She's all I've got,' the woman went on. 'I left her in the boat while I went back to cool my oven, and when I came out of the house, she was gone. Oh, she's a rascal! I haven't seen her since. I've got to sell her in the market today, or I don't eat!'

'Perhaps she didn't want to go to market,' said Bartek, not knowing what else to say to such an awful face. Then he felt sorry for her and added: 'Look, come and share my breakfast. There's nothing like breakfast in the fresh air on a morning like this.'

'True enough, there's nothing like it,' said the ugly woman, eyeing the cream cheese and warm porridge. So she climbed out of the boat while Bartek brought out another bowl, and they sat down and ate together.

'You're a very kind man and I thank you very much,' said the woman, smacking her lips. 'This is probably the last good meal I'll have for a long time if Dandy doesn't turn up. All I've got left now is a great imagination, and that won't fill my stomach.'

She went on to tell Bartek all her troubles; how she was alone in the world and found it difficult to make ends meet. Bartek in turn told her about his problem with the demon, and the more he looked at her, the uglier she seemed to become, although she had a pleasant enough way with her.

'I think I may be able to help you,' said the woman when Bartek had finished speaking. 'Yes, yes, I do believe I've got an idea.'

'Quick sticks, let's hear it!' cried Bartek. 'I've only a few more weeks left before the year is up.'

'First of all,' began the woman, 'as you can see, I'm no beauty.' Bartek nodded in agreement. 'But what I lack in looks

I've made up for by having a great imagination.'

'You've said that before,' put in Bartek impatiently.

'And I'll say it again if it pleases me,' declared the woman, 'because 'tis true, and I can use it to help you if you agree to do something for me.'

'Oh no,' thought Bartek. 'Not another bargain!' But he added aloud: 'Anything at all, just say the word.'

'I want you to marry me,' said the woman, slapping her knee.

'*Marry you?*' shrieked Bartek, toppling off his stool.

'Well, no one else will, and that's for sure,' admitted the woman. 'But so long as you don't look at me, I promise you'll have the better part of the bargain, and my name is Rhubarba.'

'How appropriate!' said Bartek, who was a plainly spoken man. 'Your ears remind me of rhubarb leaves.'

'So I believe,' agreed the woman.

'And your nose looks like an enormous carrot,' went on Bartek, hoping she would be offended and go away.

'Exactly what I think too,' came the reply.

'And your mouth – well, I don't know what it looks like,' Bartek muttered, now at a loss for comparisons.

But quick as a flash she said: 'Neither do I. I couldn't agree with you more. You see how well suited we are. Now will you marry me or won't you?'

'Yes, I will!' Bartek's answer came swiftly because he could think of nothing worse than slavery with a demon.

So they were married, and what a pleasant surprise it was for Bartek to discover that his wife was an absolute gem. How she cared for him! She never seemed to stop washing, cleaning and cooking, and she was as happy as a lark. She asked for nothing, and was more than content with very little.

As the weeks went by, Bartek would look at her and say: 'Ugly you are, my dear, even a blind man would be hard put to it to deny it, but how easy you are to please. You cost me nothing at all, and a whole cartload of gratitude I give you for that, since I'm a poor man.'

His wife would listen with her big curly ears and look at him with love in her little pin-point eyes, yet not once did she mention how she was going to save him from Rokita the forest demon.

One morning Bartek awoke and knew it was time for the demon to return. His wife was already in the kitchen making the breakfast, and Bartek began to think that after all she had deceived him into marrying her. He felt sad, because he had become extremely fond of her.

He ate his breakfast in silence and watched Rhubarba as she went into the bedroom and came out with a pillow. She tucked it under her arm and walked to the outhouse. Bartek was curious and followed her. He peeped through the door and saw that she was carefully unpicking one of the seams of the pillow. He could keep silent no longer and called out: 'What are you doing, my pet?'

'Helping you, my husband,' she replied. 'Now listen well. When the forest demon comes, I will be transformed into a rare bird. I shall be a popplesnitch. Don't forget the name – a popplesnitch.'

'Popplesnitch it shall be if you say so,' agreed Bartek, who was perplexed, but he knew his wife was the one with the great imagination. He stood transfixed, wondering what on earth she was going to do next.

Rhubarba opened up the pillow and shook the feathers out on to the floor, then, going to a corner where she had a large barrel of honey, she took off the lid and climbed inside.

'Merciful heaven! The poor dear's gone mad!' shouted Bartek, rushing forward. 'My angel, you've climbed into the honey barrel!'

'I know,' came the muffled reply.

'But you can't know or you wouldn't be in there,' insisted Bartek. 'It's honey, my precious pearl.'

His wife slowly stood up, completely glazed with thick yellow honey, and climbed out on to the floor. 'Popplesnitch,' was all she said.

'Shall I get the wash-tub ready my – er – popplesnitch?' asked Bartek uncertainly.

But Rhubarba was not listening. She squelched her way over to the heap of feathers and began to roll about among them. Feathers flew all over the place, but most of them stuck to the honey on Rhubarba, and when she stood up she was transformed. No one could possibly think she was a human being.

At that moment a voice called out: 'Bartek, are you there? Your year is over and I have come for you.'

As Bartek went out, his wife whispered to him: 'Remember I'm a popplesnitch.' He nodded and went to meet the demon, who was standing on the roof of the cottage.

'Of course you may take me,' he said with a smile. 'But only if you can name the rare bird I have in my outhouse.'

'This is wasting time,' the demon answered. 'Anyway, bring it out and I'll tell you what it is, then we must be gone. I have other things to do today.'

Bartek opened the door and out hopped the oddest-looking bird in the world. It squawked and bounded about the grass, and the demon looked on in disbelief.

'It's a . . . It's . . . It's . . .' but he could not give it a name.

'Come along now, you said you were in a hurry,' laughed Bartek. 'What is the name of this rare bird?'

'How can I know its name when there is no such bird?' exclaimed Rokita.

When the 'bird' heard that it did not exist, it began to scream with rage, and run backwards and forwards as though on the attack. It leapt up on to the roof of the well.

'Be ready to defend yourself,' shouted Bartek. 'It doubles its strength when it's angry, so watch what you say.'

'Oooh, I give up! I give up!' said Rokita hastily. 'I've never seen one of these before. I don't know what it's called.'

'Ha, ha! It's a popplesnitch!' cried Bartek triumphantly. 'Do you hear me? A popplesnitch!'

'*Popplesnitch*?' echoed the demon, and he seemed to wilt like a dry plant. He was so furious with himself that he ran off among the trees with leaps and yelps, whacking himself with his sharp tail.

Rhubarba went back into the outhouse, and her husband brought her a tub full of water to wash off her plumage. Soon she was her ugly old self again.

'Oh, my dearest wife,' smiled Bartek with a shiny tear of happiness in each eye. 'From now on you will always be the most beautiful woman imaginable to me. What a fortunate man I am.'

The next day, the black-and-white cow appeared mooing at the door, which Bartek and his wife took as a sign of good luck. So it proved to be, because he still had the splendid gun and an excellent wife, and the forest demon never troubled them again.

Onsongo and the Masai Cattle

An African tale
retold by Humphrey Harman

Akinyi was a woman of the Kisii people and she lived with her three sons high in the hills above the Great Lake. Her house was perched on a hill-top and five hundred feet below it was the stream from which each day she fetched her household water, striding upright with the heavy pot on her head and the walk of a hill woman. On either side of the stream were Akinyi's gardens, arranged in terraced steps, and here she grew her sweet potatoes and beans, her finger millet and maize and the tiny, sweet bananas called 'ladies' fingers'.

Behind the house rose up the Great Kisii Mountain, where no one lives because it is made of iron and the lightning strikes there more than any place in the world; but below it the land dropped away and away, dotted with the farms of her people, down to the Great Lake. In the morning everything would seem so clear and near that you might believe you could throw a stone on the roof of a house five miles away (of course you couldn't), but when the sun was high and everything made of polished brass they all vanished in the heat and you might have been standing on the edge of the world.

Akinyi was a widow. Her husband had been killed by a leopard who had come in the night and stolen a goat. The man had taken a spear and gone out in the morning and never come home again alive. But the leopard skin hung in Akinyi's house and there were three great spear holes in it.

So then Akinyi had her sons to look after, because she had not bothered to marry again, and although she worked hard in her garden they remained poor.

The three brothers were called Onsongo (the eldest), Otinga and Opio and when they were small they were as like as puppies in a basket but when they were older they grew apart.

Otinga and Opio were good Kisii boys with deep chests and muscley legs (it comes from running up and down hills), and they herded their mother's tiny flock of goats and practised throwing spears with the other boys, and the old Kisii men looked at them with approval.

'Eh, a handsome pair,' they said. 'It's a pity the family's so poor. With a good herd of cattle to help, either boy would make a fine son-in-law. Well, it's servants of richer men they'll have to be all their lives . . . and then, of course, there's the eldest, Onsongo. Tch, tch! It's hard what some folks have to put up with.'

And then, of course, there was Onsongo.

He was fat and sleepy and they said he was lazy. Perhaps he was. Certainly the things he did drove poor Akinyi to despair. Send him to weed a garden and you'd find him sitting in the shade playing with a bit of clay he had scooped out of the stream. And the hoe lying in the beans and not a thing done. When his mother screamed at him he'd look up with placid sleepy eyes and say: 'Eh! I'm sorry, Mama. I forgot.'

Forgot! How can one forget to weed a garden when you're sitting in it?

Send him to watch the goats and you'd find him scraping away at a bit of wood with his knife and the goats eating a neighbour's young corn.

'I'm sorry, Mama, I forgot.'

Then Akinyi would lose all patience and take a little stick to improve his memory, but it never did much good and afterwards she would feel sorry and cry and say: 'Onsongo, Onsongo! Aren't things difficult enough without you behaving like this?'

And Onsongo would also be sorry (he really was), and promise to try and do better, and mean it because he loved his mother and set off with the best of intentions until . . . until he forgot again.

He was hopeless.

The other boys and girls made up songs about Onsongo in the way that Africans do, that is, all together, on the spur of the moment, and never write them down. It's the best way to do it because only the good ones get remembered. A group of them would find him sleeping in the grass. They would gather round on tip-toe and sing softly over the body, answering each other.

The song would finish, as you'll see, with a great shout and screams of laughter and Onsongo would wake up with a jump and stare at them in surprise. Then (and this was the nicest thing about him) he would smile and wander away absent-mindedly, not in the smallest bit angry. No one could ever make Onsongo cross and he'd never been known to lose his temper. In fact he was the most even-tempered young man for miles around. Nothing seemed to upset him.

This is the song the boys and girls sang:

Is Otinga here?	He's away on the hillside.
Is Opio here?	He's below in the valley.
Well, is Onsongo here?	Sh!
Is he asleep or awake?	Asleep.

See how he curls in the grass like a hyrax,[1]

A spider has made a web between his toes.

Tell him the buck are in his garden.	He yawns.
Tell him the rats are in the store.	He sighs.
Tell him his house is burnt down.	He's . . .
Is he?	Yes, he's asleep again!
	WAKE UP!
	Onsongo
	friend

dear

   our

     make

  we

shall

how

Oh,

Onsongo was not really lazy or rather, not always lazy. His trouble was that he could only do the things he liked doing and that what he called work serious people called play. He was in fact an artist.

As a little boy he took the red clay which the white ants used to make their tall houses and out of this he shaped bulls and hares, men and women, as many of the other children did when they were alone all day with the goats and had to find their own toys. No one took any notice of this, it was only a little boy playing, but if they had done they would have noticed that his bulls were more bull-like than other children's and that his hares crouched exactly as they do before they run doubling through the grass. You could almost see their noses twitching.

---

[1] Hyrax: a small, sleepy animal like a hamster, also known as a 'rock-rabbit.'

When he was older he carved in wood or, best of all, in the fat white soapstone which could be found in the hills and which cut like cheese when it was first dug but later grew hard. The Kisii had always hollowed their pipe bowls from this with a long reed for the stem. But Onsongo made new pipes. What pipes! Pipes like a bird with a curved beak, a zebra's head, an old man with a beard or a woman carrying a pot. And to the Kisii there seemed a magic in these things, so that a man longed to own one and tobacco tasted better for being smoked in them.

When Akinyi had given up trying to turn him into a serious person and let him alone, he made things all day. Pipe bowls and wooden drums with buck leaping and running all over them, stools with snakes and lizards curling up their legs, and figures of men and animals which people were half afraid to touch because it seemed that here was a cleverness a little more than human.

But of course it was only Onsongo. Fat, smiling, harmless Onsongo whose hands were ever at useless things, who made the stone and the wood and the clay alive.

Wah!

Sometimes when an old man praised a pipe he had begged or a stool he had exchanged for a basket of grain Akinyi looked at her eldest son with troubled pride and then sighed. It is not always very comfortable having an artist in the family.

'Doing this is all very well,' she said, 'and brings in an occasional goat or chicken. But to get on, a man must have cattle to buy land and marry a wife. Cattle. That's what a young man should turn his mind to, not carving. And if he has no rich father to start him off in the right way then he must take his chance with other young men, raiding neighbouring tribes and earning cattle with his spear and cunning.'

Akinyi sighed. Onsongo showed no sign of ever doing that.

Until he met Anyika.

She was a girl from a village a few miles away and pretty enough for six. Plenty of young men were anxious to marry Anyika but, whoever it was, he was going to have to be rich, for her father was demanding a great price for the privilege of marrying into the family.

Onsongo met her at the marriage of a relative, and after that it was noticed that he often stirred himself to walk to Anyika's village. Anyika's parents also noticed that a plague of carved animals began to litter the house, one was continually stumbling over a stone crocodile or sitting on a wooden bull, and sometimes it hurt.

For Onsongo was in love with Anyika and when he could not be with her he calmed his feelings by a fury of carving and then presented the finished objects to her.

As for Anyika, she said little, for she was not a talkative girl, but she always seemed glad to see him and now and then, when she thought no one was watching, she picked up one of the carvings he had given her and looked at it tenderly and sadly.

One day Onsongo was working happily when a handsome young man, a son of a rich neighbour, stopped beside him.

'Make me a stool, Onsongo,' he said. 'It must be a good one and I'll pay you five goats for it. I'm going to marry Anyika and I need something as a present for her father.'

'Then I won't make it,' replied Onsongo indignantly, 'because I'm going to marry her myself.' (It was very strange, but he had only just discovered that he was going to do this.)

'You!' said the young neighbour. 'Where're you going to get the cattle for the dowry? From the Masai?'

And he laughed and strolled on.

Onsongo put down his tools and ran the whole way to Anyika's house.

'Anyika,' he said, 'let's get married. I'll go and ask your father.'

'Oh Onsongo,' replied Anyika, 'I wish we could, I'd give anything in the world for that to happen but . . . but where are you going to get the cattle for the dowry?'

But Onsongo was on his way to Anyika's father. The old man was not unkind and he had known Onsongo's father, but he thought the boy a fool and could never really consider him as a serious person at all. He slowly and patiently explained that before Anyika could get married a large dowry must be paid. He expected it, so did his family and his clan. It was customary.

'How much?' asked Onsongo.

'Forty cows.'

This was a figure that should have taken Onsongo's breath

away, but he was not a very practical man and, anyway, the thought of marrying Anyika made him feel that he was floating about twelve inches from the ground and not at all inclined to bother about cows.

'Good,' he replied absent-mindedly. 'I'll see about it.'

'Eh? One moment,' said the father. 'I think we'd better settle on a definite time, eh? Let's say payment in full in a month's time. That should show the offer's serious.'

'As you like,' murmured Onsongo, who was off to tell his mother.

'Eh!' squeaked the old man with astonishment. He knew just how poor Onsongo was. 'Where are you going to get them from, the Masai?'

But Onsongo was gone.

'Mother,' he announced when he got home, 'I'm going to marry Anyika!'

The old woman sat down and looked at her son. She didn't know whether to laugh or cry.

'Oh, Onsongo, Onsongo,' she said, 'and where will people like us find all the cows to pay the dowry of a girl like Anyika? How many do you think it would need?'

'I know you always think that I'm unpractical,' said Onsongo, 'but I'm not. I found out about that. I asked her father. He'll be glad to have me as a son-in-law for forty cows.'

His mother laughed.

'Forty cows! Forty! It might as well be forty stars. How do you think you will find them? Where'll you get them from, the Masai?'

This was the third time that day that Onsongo had been asked this question and he was getting tired of it. It seemed to him that people were putting difficulties in his way. And then he hadn't really thought about all those cattle, his head had been too full of the wonderful idea of marrying Anyika. He considered them now. It occurred to him that the two things were connected, he couldn't marry Anyika without the cattle. And the whole family hadn't a single cow. Or much likelihood of getting one.

A great depression filled Onsongo. Other young men had

cattle. Beefy, stupid young men, all muscle and bounce, who could throw spears and whose idea of a good time was to walk forty miles over the borders of Kisii, steal a cow and run for their miserable lives.

Bah!

His mother wondered if he had heard what she said. He so often didn't.

'Where'll you get them from, Onsongo?' she asked gently. 'The Masai?'

Then Onsongo got up in a great temper.

'Yes, Mother,' he said with enormous dignity. 'That's exactly what I will do!'

And he stalked out.

It sounded well. When his brothers came home and heard all about it from their mother they asked Onsongo the same question and got the same answer. This time it was put differently. They had not known him so angry before, he never lost his temper when people made fun of him, and so they were a little afraid. The next few days he sat playing with a piece of wood, deep in thought, or he might have been asleep. They watched him curiously and after a while they let him alone.

Onsongo thought and thought.

'Where will you get them from, Onsongo, the Masai?'

The Masai were people, and they lived on the plain that began when the Kisii Mountains ended, and it was fortunate for the Kisii that their hills were steep and that the Masai hated hills. Otherwise they would have been brushed into the lake like crumbs being shaken out of a window.

The Masai were that sort of people.

Their warriors were tall, wore great head-dresses of ostrich feathers and painted their bodies red. They loved cattle and grazed great herds on the plain.

The other thing they loved was war, and for a thousand miles in every direction they were the terror of Africa: they raided and burned and stole and killed. Only where people lived in forests and on the steep hills were they safe from the Masai, providing that they had nowhere else to go, were desperate and fought hard for their homes.

When a baby was naughty and wearied his mother with crying she would say: 'Hush, my darling, or the Masai will hear you.'

Then, if the child was old enough to understand, he behaved.

'Where will you get the cattle from, Onsongo, the Masai?'

After a week Onsongo seemed to get over his sulks and began to work at making things again, whistling softly as he did so. His brothers were tactful and pretended that the whole thing had not happened. And after a while they forgot that it had. His mother, who remembered and felt sorry for him, asked him what he was making and in answer he held up a half-finished hunting horn. It was a long ox horn and, having hollowed it out and cut the tip off for a mouthpiece, Onsongo was slowly and carefully thinning the walls until they were as fragile as an egg-shell. You could see the light through them.

'If you make them so thin they will easily break,' she said.

'It doesn't matter,' said Onsongo. 'It only has to be used once.'

After that he refused to talk any more about it. Until one morning when the horn was finished Onsongo called his mother and his brothers and announced: 'Now we're going to get my cattle from the Masai so that I can marry Anyika. Opio and Otinga, you'd better get ready for the journey because I'll need help.'

'I should just imagine you will, brother,' said Otinga. 'A great deal of it. Unfortunately, you'll have to get it somewhere else. I'd prefer to stay alive than be spoken of as a hero. Opio, of course, can speak for himself.'

'Yes,' said Opio hurriedly. 'I . . . I thought about making . . . making . . . eh . . . making a new garden. On the other side of the stream. It will take about . . . How long will your cattle raid last, brother?'

'About four days,' said Onsongo.

'Well, the garden will take about that time. It ought to be done before the rains come, so if you don't mind . . .'

Then Onsongo lost his temper.

'Listen to me,' he shouted. 'All my life I've been told that the proper thing for a man to be was a warrior, and run and throw spears and leap about the place like a bull wildebeest, when all I wanted to do was to be left alone to make things. Well, I left it to you two. You were the warriors of the family and should have been stealing cattle. But you haven't. There's not a cow to bless ourselves with, much less get married on, so I've got to do something about it. And now you won't even help. What in heaven's name was the use of all this poking about with spears in the past?'

Akinyi stopped her son.

'Onsongo,' she asked, 'are you serious?'

'Yes, Mother, of course I am.'

'And have you got a plan?'

'Yes, Mother and I'm sure it will work.'

'If I came could I be of any help?'

'Ye-e-s. It'll be more difficult than it would be if we had these two oafs with us and we shan't get so many cattle but –'

Here, of course, Opio and Otinga protested that their mother couldn't go raiding cattle against the Masai, and Onsongo made some wounding remarks about recruiting the village grandmothers since the young men had to dig their gardens, and Akinyi said quietly, but very firmly, that she was going, and of course Opio and Otinga said that they would too.

Which is what Akinyi had meant them to say.

Then all their heads drew together and Onsongo explained his plan. And presently, Opio laughed and hitched nearer and Otinga said slowly: 'Yes, yes, of course!'

The very next day they set off for the plain, a day's hard walk away. They took with them enough food for a few days and a length of slender hide rope. The younger brothers carried hunting spears. Onsongo took his horn.

That night they slept on the top of the last steep slope that fell to the plain , and in the morning when they had breakfasted on cold maize cake they moved along the hillside until they saw what they were looking for. Below them was a water-hole, little more than a small pond in a sea of mud churned up by the feet of cattle and the whole surrounded by dry reeds and a few trees. It was the end of the long dry season and water on the plain would be scarce. The marks of cattle were fresh; the Masai were using this pool.

However, no one was there at the moment and Opio and Otinga went down to catch a crested crane, which was an important part of their plan.

They did it very neatly with a long noose made from the hide rope. They laid this out on the ground with a handful of grain scattered inside the noose for bait, and then hid in the reeds with the free end of the rope. There were many cranes nearby, for in the dry season they stay close to water, and when they saw the boys disappear into the reeds they came flying over to see what was happening. Cranes are as curious as cows about anything new going on.

Then one of them stepped with jerky strides into the noose and stabbed at the grain, and Opio jerked the rope from the

reeds and they caught him by his long nobbly legs. He lay on his back and screamed furiously: 'Kerwonk!' and then they gathered him up and tied the wings and also put another piece of rope round that beak to stop him stabbing at them (a crane's beak is no joke). Then they carried him up the hill and settled down in the grass to watch the water-hole.

They were tired after their journey of the day before and under the hot sun they all fell asleep. When they woke it was late afternoon and the Masai had arrived. They counted ten young warriors, three standing on one leg apiece like storks, watching more than a hundred fine cows drink at the pool, the others lazing on their backs in the reeds or polishing their long spears with wisps of dry grass.

The four Kisii watched with their hearts beating faster. After the cows had been watered they crowded together near the water for the night. The Masai lit a fire and gathered round it, leaving two men to watch the cattle. The watchers guessed that what they were seeing happened every night.

In the morning the Masai drove the cattle across the plain out of sight, but in a different direction from yesterday. When they were gone Akinyi and her three sons ate a little food, and then they untied the crane's beak and gave the furious bird some food and water. After that they waited all day, but this time they were careful not to go to sleep.

When it was evening they saw, far away, a cloud of dust moving and this they knew was the cattle being driven back to water. Then all four of them slipped quickly down to where, a half a mile beyond the pool and on the other side to where the cattle slept, there was a solitary Mukubu tree, whose smooth grey bark was covered in long thorns. They helped Onsongo to climb this, and when he was over the thorns they handed him up the tied crane and the horn. With these he disappeared into the dense leaves so that no one could have told a man was there. The other three went back to the pool and hid among the reeds.

The cattle came near and broke into a run when they smelt the water. Then the bellowing stopped as they reached the water. The Masai herdsmen followed. From close by they were a

frightening sight: tall young men with faces like cruel masks and their hair arranged in plaits and dyed red. The long spears looked terrible. Opio, Otinga and Akinyi trembled and tried to forget all the shocking stories they had heard of the Masai. What Onsongo thought and how he behaved no one knows, because he was alone, but presently from the tree in which he was hidden there came the long hoarse roar of the horn. Onsongo blew it three times and then finished the performance with a cluster of little graceful notes. Then there was silence.

The Masai pricked up their ears. They took their spears, and leaving two of their number there lounged off round the pool and across the plain to where they judged the noise had come from. They were not suspicious, only idle and curious in a bored kind of way.

They were casting round rather like a pack of gaunt red hunting dogs when the horn blew again. It was a gentle sound now and almost seemed to talk. The Masai gathered at the foot of the tree and gazed up. There was nothing to be seen, no explanation at all of the noise.

They puzzled over it. One or two eyed the thorns lazily and decided against climbing up.

Their two companions at the pool called questions to them.

'Come and see,' they shouted back from the tree and the two herdsmen glanced at the cattle. They were all drinking, soft noses lowered to the water, blowing quietly, mild eyes almost closed. They would finish drinking and then settle down where they slept each night. Nothing could happen. The two herdsmen skirted the reeds and joined their friends speculating beneath the trees.

As they arrived the horn blew again, three great blasts.

'It's a wizard,' said the Masai.

'Nonsense, it's a bird.'

'Oh, listen to the man. A bird! Whoever heard the like of that noise made by a bird?'

'It's Chemosit, brother, who is half man and half bird. If we wait until night we'll see his mouth shining red.' (Chemosit was a particularly unpleasant devil in whom the Masai believed).

'Climb up there, Seriani. Climb up and tell us what it is.'

'Not I. Not with Chemosit standing up there on one leg with his great mouth gobbling behind the leaves. Besides, the thorns are sharp.'

The horn blew softly.

'Listen to it. Trying to tempt one of us up.'

'Bah, that's neither a bird or Chemosit. It sounds like a horn.'

'Eh! Have you ever heard a horn blow itself?'

The horn howled harshly.

'There, listen to it. It's Chemosit and now he's angry because his plan has failed and no one has gone up.'

And while they stood there, lazily babbling in the dusk, on the other side of the reeds Opio, Otinga and Akinyi gathered together the cattle and, unseen, drove them away to the hills.

It was as easy as that.

From the tree Onsongo watched them go. He listened with half his mind to the Masai exercising their imagination below, the rest of him was trying to judge the best time for the next move. His brothers and the cattle had now disappeared into the evening haze. They would be in the hills and with a long start. In half an hour it would be dark and impossible to follow them. Even if they could see their tracks not even the Masai would go wandering at night through the Kisii hills after a raiding party whose size they did not know.

Onsongo decided that now was the time.

He blew on the horn three times with all his strength. His brothers heard those notes distantly and knew what they meant. They hurried on, sweating, whispering to the cows and tapping their flanks gently with the butts of their spears.

Then, hidden by the leaves, Onsongo tied the horn to the leg of the crane, untied the bird's wings and beak and set it loose.

It jumped out of the leaves, and flapped indignantly over the gaping Masai, the horn dangling from its leg. Then it opened its beak, shouted furiously: 'Kerwonk!' and flew off clumsily.

The Masai stared after it.

'I said it was a bird!'

'Did you see the horn? That's no bird. It's a magician in the shape of a bird.'

'And the horn's a magic horn!'

And they all set off like the wind across the plain after the crane to capture the magic horn, for the bird, hampered by the horn, kept landing and hopping round on one leg and then flying on, swearing.

The Masai chased it for a while before it vanished in the darkness. Then they came back to the pool and found every cow gone.

Eh!

And of course while all this was going on Onsongo got out of that tree and ran to the hills as fast as his short fat legs would carry him. He wasn't built for running, but just then he had an excellent reason for it and he did quite well.

He joined his mother and his brothers in the hills and they reached home safely with more cattle than any of their neighbours had ever seen before.

And that is really the end of the story.

Onsongo married his Anyika and very happy they were, although sometimes she used to complain that he was lazy.

Then Onsongo would rouse himself and look at her indignantly.

'Lazy! Me? Bah, I was thinking. Thinking, woman! Do you know what that means? What I did when I got the cattle from the Masai. Brains are better than brawn any day!'

And he would stalk off and be found sleepily carving a piece of wood ten minutes later, his temper quite restored.

The crane? He flew to a tree for the night and the thong that held the horn broke and set him free. The horn lodged in the crook of a branch and the next year a tiny red-capped bird, whose name I have forgotten, made a nest inside and reared five splendid children.

As for Akinyi, she lived to be a hundred and nine, and became the most famous old woman in the whole history of the Kisii tribe.

The Black Thief

an Irish tale
retold by Eileen O'Faolain

King Conal's Horses

Long ago in Erin there was a king, and he was married to a queen who was beautiful and kind. So kind was she that she was beloved by all the people of the land, especially the poor who came daily to the palace looking for help. Now this king and queen had three fine sons, and they were the happiest family in Erin until the day the queen took sick with a strange disease. Knowing she was going to die, the queen called the king to her bedside and said to him:

'If I die and you marry again, promise me you will send my three sons away to a distant part of the kingdom, so that they may not be under the control of a strange woman, until they come to manhood.'

The king gave her his word that he would carry out her wishes and then the queen died peacefully. The king mourned her sadly for a year or two, and never thought of taking another wife, until his councillors told him he should marry again for the good of the realm. He ordered a castle then to be built in a far distant part of his kingdom, and there he sent his three sons with servants and teachers to look after them. Then he married again and was happy once more until his new wife had a son.

One day, shortly after the birth of his new son, the king was out hunting, and the queen went for a walk around the castle grounds. As she passed by the cottage of a half-crazy old hen-wife she heard the old woman complaining of her neglect of the poor, and shouting out after her as she passed by:

'It is little you care for the poor and the needy who live by your grand castle walls, not like the fine generous queen your husband had before you. It was she was the grand lady that would take the cloak off her own back and give it to them that wanted it more.'

Hearing her, the young queen stopped to ask about the dead queen, and promising the old woman a hundred speckled goats, a hundred sheep and a hundred cows to tell her all, she heard from her of the three sons the king had in the distant castle on the far side of his kingdom. 'And,' said the old woman, 'when they come of age your son will not have a place to lay his head, no more than the birds of the air.'

As she listened to the old hen-wife the young queen began to sorrow for the fate of her son, but the old woman comforted her:

'Listen to me and I will tell you how to get rid of the king's three sons. Get the king to bring them back to the castle for a visit, and while they are there, challenge each one of them, one after the other, to a game of chess. I will give you an enchanted board to play on that will make you win. When you have won from the three of them, tell them that you put as a sentence on them that they should go for the three steeds of King Conal, and bring them back to you, as you want to ride three times around the boundaries of the kingdom. They will go, and you will never see them again, for many is the champion that went seeking King Conal's horses and never came back again. Then your own son will be king when the time comes.'

The queen went home, and that very evening when the king rode back from the hunt she asked him about his sons, and why he kept them away from her.

'Bring them back home,' she begged him, 'and you will see that I will be as fond of them as I am of my own son.'

So the king brought his three sons home, and had a great feast prepared to welcome them, and all the people of the country were delighted to see them back once more.

After the feast the queen challenged each brother, one after the other, to a game of chess. She played three games with each one, she won two from each, and pretended to lose the third.

That night the eldest son came to her and said: 'What sentence will you put on me and my brothers for having lost to you?'

'I put you and your two brothers under bonds not to sleep twice in the same house, or eat twice at the same table, until you bring me the three steeds of King Conal, as I want to ride three times around the boundaries of the kingdom.'

'Where, O Queen, will we find the horses of King Conal?' asked the eldest brother.

'There are four quarters in the world,' said the queen, 'and you will surely find him in one of them.'

'I will give you your sentence now,' said the eldest brother, 'for the game that you lost to us. I put you under bonds of enchantment to stand on the top of the castle, and stay there without coming down, and watch for us till we come back with the horses.'

'Remove from me your sentence; I will remove mine,' said the queen.

'If a young man is relieved of the first sentence that is put on him he will never do any good,' said the king's son. 'We will go for the horses.'

Next day the three brothers said farewell to their father and set out to find the castle of King Conal. After travelling for many days and getting no tidings of the place they were seeking, they came up with a lame man who was wearing a black cap on his head.

'Who are you, what brought you to these parts, and where are you bound for?' asked the man of the black cap as he stood in front of them.

'We are the three sons of the King of Erin,' said the eldest of the three brothers, 'and we are looking for the three horses of King Conal to bring back to our stepmother.'

'Come and spend the night with me,' said the lame stranger, 'and tomorrow I will go with you and be your guide to King Conal's castle.'

So as dusk was falling the three brothers went with the stranger, and passed the night in his house. Next morning the man in the black cap called them early, and told them that trying to get

King Conal's horses was a thing that had cost many a brave champion his life. 'But,' he said, 'I will help you, and maybe we will succeed, though without my help you would have no chance at all.'

So the four of them set out once more, and before nightfall they reached the castle of King Conal. They waited until the middle of the night before they went to the stables for the horses, and then great was their joy to find that all the guards were sound asleep.

The three brothers and the man with the black cap seized their chance and took a horse each and began to mount, but as soon as they touched them the horses reared up madly and began to neigh and whinny so loudly that they woke up the whole castle. The guards rushed on the three brothers and seized them at once with the man in the black cap and brought them before King Conal.

King Conal sat on a massive throne of gold in the great hall of the castle. At each side of him and all around the back of his throne stood his guards with drawn swords. In front of him was a great cauldron of oil boiling and bubbling over a blazing fire.

'Ah,' said King Conal, when he saw the man in the black cap in front of him, 'only that the Black Thief is dead, I'd say you were he.'

'I am the Black Thief,' said the man in the black cap.

'Indeed,' said the King, 'we'll soon find that out. And who are these three young men?'

'We are the three sons of the King of Erin,' said the brothers.

'Now,' said King Conal, 'we'll begin on the youngest. But stir up the fire there under the cauldron, for the oil is gone off the boil.'

Then the King turned to the Black Thief and said:

'Now, isn't that young man very near death this minute?'

'I was nearer death once,' said the Black Thief, 'and I escaped.'

'Tell me the story,' said King Conal, 'and if it's a thing that you were nearer death than he is this minute, I will let him go with his life.'

'That's a bargain,' said the Black Thief, and he began to tell King Conal the story.

The Three Enchanted Maidens

'When I was a young man I had lands and riches in plenty, and I lived in ease and comfort until three witches came and destroyed my property. Then I took to the roads and became a famous thief, the most famous that ever lived in Erin, the Black Thief.

'Now, these three witches were three daughters of a king that was in Erin at that time, and they were three of the most beautiful maidens in Erin during the daytime, but at night, because of a spell a wizard put on them, they changed into three hideous hags.

'Now it happened, before I lost my property and took to the roads, that I had my men cut and bring in for me a supply of turf to last me seven years. The great reek was raised outside my house, and it was so big, that it looked like a black mountain. Well, late one night – after midnight it was – I was coming home from a banquet, and what did I see but the three ugly witches taking the turf from my reek and loading it into three creels on their backs and making off with it. That winter they never stopped taking it until they made off with every bit of turf I had.

'The next season I laid in enough turf again to last me for

seven years, but the witches came once more and took it off with them. Then one night I watched while they filled their creels, and I followed them into the hills, and there I saw them go down into an underground passage in the rocks, twenty fathoms deep in the ground.

'I looked down, and there I saw them below with a whole bullock in a pot and they boiling it over a great fire. I glanced around me for something to throw at them, and seeing a huge boulder near the mouth of the hole I heaved it and rolled it over till it crashed down on them below. It broke their pot and spilled their broth into the ashes of the fire.

'I took to my heels then, but soon the three witches were close behind me. I climbed a high tree to escape them, but they saw me and stopped underneath to look up at me through the branches. The eldest of the three hags then turned the second hag into a sharp axe, and the third into a fierce swift hound. Then, taking the axe, she began to cut down the tree underneath me.

'With the first blow of the axe the witch cut the tree-trunk a third of the way across. She gave a second blow and cut another third of it. Then she raised the axe for the third and last blow, but just at that moment a cock crowed, and before my eyes the axe turned into a beautiful maiden, the hag, who was felling the tree, into another beautiful maiden, and the fierce swift hound into a third. Then, joining hands, the three sisters walked away, as happy and innocent-looking as any three young maidens in Erin.

'Now,' said the Black Thief to King Conal, 'wasn't I nearer death that time than this young man is now?'

'Indeed you were,' said the king, 'but we'll have his brother instead of him. The oil is on the boil now; so there's no need to delay.'

'Even so,' said the Black Thief, 'I was once nearer death than he is this minute.'

'Let us hear the story of it,' said King Conal, 'and if you were, we will let him go with his life, too.'

The Black Thief then began his second story.

The Thirteen Enchanted Cats

'After I had broken the pot of the three witches that had stolen my turf and my cattle, they killed all my hens, and trampled my crops, and left me so poor that I had to take to the roads as a thief to make a living for my wife and family.

'One night I was driving an old horse and cow home to feed my children when I got so tired from walking behind them that I had to sit down under a tree in a thick wood to rest myself. It was cold, and as I had a flint in my pocket I lit a bit of a fire to keep the heat in me. I wasn't long sitting by the fire when I saw, stealing around me out of the darkness, thirteen of the biggest and fiercest-looking cats that ever were seen within the walls of the world. Twelve of them were each the size of a fully grown man, but the thirteenth, their leader, was the size of any two of them put together. He was a great, powerful cat with fiery green eyes that shone and sparkled as he sat in front of the fire facing me. The others sat six at each side of him, and they began to purr together, making a noise like thunder in the still night air.

'After a while the big red one raised up his head and looked across the fire at me and said:

' "I won't be hungry any longer; give me something to eat at once."

' "I have nothing to give you, unless you take that old white horse tethered to the tree over there behind you."

'The red cat made a spring at the horse and, making two halves of him, ate one half himself, and left the other to his twelve comrades. They tore it to pieces and picked every bone clean.

'Then the thirteen of them came back to the fire again, and sat around me, licking their lips and purring with a noise like thunder. After a while the big cat spoke again and said:

' "I'm hungry again; give me some more to eat."

' "I have nothing to give you, unless you take the cow without horns," I answered.

'The red cat made for the cow and made two halves of her, as he did with the horse. One half he ate himself and the other half he left to his twelve comrades. While the fierce cats were eating the cow, I took off my coat, wrapped it around a log, and put my cap on top of it to make it look like myself, for I knew what they would do next. Then I quickly climbed the tree overhead.

'Soon the cats had finished every scrap of the old cow and they came back and sat around the fire once more. Then looking at the block of wood that I had put in place of myself, the red cat spoke again:

' "Have you any more food for me, for I am starving this minute?"

'The block of wood gave no answer, so the leader of the cats sprang across the fire at it and began to bite and tear it with his claws. But he soon found out his mistake.

' "Ah," he said, "so you are gone. But we will soon find you, no matter how well you have hidden yourself."

'Then he called on his twelve cats to go out all over Erin and search for me, six to go under the ground and six over the ground. He himself sat down under the tree. In a short time the cats, having searched the whole country from top to bottom, came back without finding a trace of me. It was then he chanced to look up into the tree and see me. "Aha," he said, "there you are. I'll soon have you down out of that. Come," he said to the twelve cats, "and gnaw down that tree."

'The twelve cats got around the trunk of the tree then and started to gnaw it across, and it wasn't long before they had it cut through, bringing it crashing down flat on the ground before their leader. But just as it fell I managed to spring on to the branches of the tree next to it. Then they started to gnaw that one down, and at the last moment before it fell, I escaped on to the tree next to that. And so all night they kept on after me, gnawing down each tree I was hiding in, until at last I had reached the very last tree of the forest. Then they started to gnaw that one down, and I did not know what way to escape them now. They had it half gnawed across when who should come along but thirteen terrible wolves, a pack of twelve, and a great fierce wolf who was their leader.

'The wolves charged the cats, and fierce and bloody was the fight between them, until at last the twelve cats and the twelve wolves were all stretched out dead and only the two leaders fought on. Then the leader of the wolves made a fierce snap at the red cat, but the red cat lashed the wolf's head with his tail and made two halves of it. The two of them then fell dead on top of one another. Then I was able to come down out of the tree and go home, but as I climbed down it swayed and creaked under me, for it was cut nearly through.

'Now,' said the Black Thief, 'was I not nearer death that time than this young man?'

'Indeed you were so,' said King Conal, 'and he may go with his life, for I'll not break my word. But I'll have the third one yet, so heat up the oil there, and make it good and hot.'

Then he said, 'Were you ever nearer death than this young man?'

'I was to be sure,' said the Black Thief.

'Tell me about it,' said King Conal, 'and if you were I'll let him go free like his brothers.'

Then the Black Thief told King Conal the third story.

The Faithless Apprentice

'Some time after practising my trade for a while I had got so clever at it that I took some apprentices to learn it from me,' said the Black Thief. 'Among them there was one young man who was cleverer than all the rest, so I spent most of my time teaching him, for he was quick and eager to learn. After a time I had taught him all I knew and he became a better thief than I was myself.

'About this time there was a giant living in a rocky den at the other end of the country, and as he pillaged and stole from all the great nobles around it was well known that this den was full of gold and riches of all kinds. So I plotted with my apprentice to go one day and get as much of his treasure as we could carry away with us. We set out, and after travelling for many days we reached the giant's den in the mountains. It was an underground cavern in the rocks, and there was only one way into it, and that was down through a deep, dark funnel in the rocks, like a chimney.

'We watched the giant for a few days, and he used to go out every morning and come back in the evening with a bag on his back that we felt sure was full of gold and jewels. One morning when the giant had left I tied a rope around the waist of my apprentice and began to lower him down through the hole in the rock leading to the giant's den. But when he was half-way down he began to shout and scream at me to draw him up again. I drew him up and then he told me that he was afraid to go down. "Go down yourself," he said, "and I'll take charge of the rope and haul you up again."

'I went down, and when I reached the giant's den I saw great yellow heaps of gold, and shining white heaps of silver and precious stones. I opened the bag and put into it as much as one man could lift, and I sent it up on the rope to my apprentice. Then I called up to him to send down the rope for myself. At first I got no answer but then he shouted down to me:

' "I am finished my apprenticeship now, for I am a better thief than yourself, and you have no more to teach me. Good-bye now, and I hope you'll have a pleasant evening with the giant."

'Then I heard no more from him. I looked now for some way of climbing out of the giant's den, but there was no way of escaping, for not even a fly could get a foothold on those steep, slippery rocks. After that I saw a heap of dead bodies in one corner of the kitchen. I threw myself down among them, for there was nowhere to hide, and I stretched out pretending I was dead.

'In the evening the giant came back carrying three more bodies. He threw the three bodies on the heap near me, and began to light a fire at the other end of the kitchen, and when it was lighted he hung a great black cauldron of water over it. Then he got a big basket and came down and filled it up with bodies. I was the first he threw in, and he put six others on top of me. He took the basket over to the pot, and turned it upside down on top of it, so that the six bodies fell into the boiling water, but I managed to hang on to the bottom of the basket. Then he laid it face downward in a corner of the kitchen, so I was safe for that time.

'When the giant had eaten his supper he fell fast asleep in the chair. Now I took my chance and crept out from underneath the basket. I went over to the entrance to the den, and there, as luck would have it, I saw the giant's ladder, that he had forgotten to turn around. It was cut out of a tree trunk, and when he had gone up or come down, all he had to do was to turn the steps around and nobody, unless someone as strong as himself, could use it. Up I climbed, and it took me no time at all to reach the top.

'And don't you think I was nearer death that time than this young man here?'

'By my troth you were near enough to it,' said the king. 'So I will pardon him along with his brothers. But it is your own turn now, and maybe it is yourself that I will put into the pot in the heel of the hunt, for I'd say you were never nearer death than you are this minute.'

'Near as I am,' said the Black Thief, 'there was a time when I was nearer.'

'When was that?' asked the king. 'Tell me about it, and maybe I'll let you go free, too, with the others.'

Then the Black Thief told the story of how he escaped from the three giants.

The Three Giants

'One day,' said the Black Thief, 'I felt tired and hungry, and coming to a house I went in to ask for refreshment. Inside I saw a young woman with a child on her lap. The young woman had a knife in her hand, and she was thrusting it at the child as if she would stab it. The beautiful child was laughing and crowing with delight, but the woman was weeping bitterly.

' "Why are you pointing the knife at the child like that?" I asked her, "and why are you crying so sorrowfully?"

'Then she told me her story:

' "Last year, when I was at a fair with my mother and father, three giants suddenly rushed in among the crowds of people. So surprised was everyone to see them that the man who had a bite in his hand did not raise it to his mouth, and the man who had a bite in his mouth did not swallow it. The giants robbed everyone of all they had, and they snatched me away from my father and mother and brought me here to this place. I was told that I was to marry the eldest giant, but I bound him not to marry me till I was eighteen years of age. I will be that in a few days, and then there will be no escape for me unless someone kills the three giants before then."

' "But why are you trying to stab the young child here?" I asked.

' "Yesterday they brought in this child and told me he was the son of a king. They gave him to me, and asked that I make a pie of him and have it ready for their supper this evening."

' "Do not kill the child," said I. "I have a young pig here that you can put into the pie, and they will not know the difference, for the flesh of a pig is very like the flesh of a child. Let us cut off one joint of the child's little finger to put in the pie, and if they are in any doubt you can show them that.''

'So the maiden did as I bade her, and made the pie with the young pig, and I went to hide in the cellar. The three giants ate the pie with great relish, each saying it was a very good pie but there was not enough of it. The eldest brother then sent the youngest giant down to the cellar to bring up a slice from one of the bodies there, as he was still hungry. The giant came down, and catching a hold of me, cut a large slice off my leg, above the knee. This pleased the eldest brother so much that he came down himself to take me up and broil me before the fire. He caught me up and threw me over his back, but he hadn't gone far when I plunged my knife deep in his heart, and he fell down dead on the floor under me.

'Then the second brother came down to get more to eat also, and he again took me on his back, but I stabbed him, too, and stretched him on the floor, like his brother.

'The youngest brother, who was still waiting at the table for some more to eat, now grew angry, and came down to see what was keeping his two brothers. Seeing them stretched on the floor, he shook them and found they were both dead. He looked around him with surprise, and he noticed me looking at him. He dashed towards me, swinging his great iron club over his head. He aimed for my head and brought the club down with such force that it dug itself into the ground to the depth of a man's knee. But I had stepped aside quickly, and not a hair of my head was hurt. While he was trying to pull his club out of the ground I ran at him, and stabbed him three times in the side. Again he raised the club and aimed a blow at me, but again I stepped aside, and now once more, while he was trying to free his club, I thrust my knife three times into his stomach. But the third time he made for me with his club, a wicked hook of it caught in me and tore a great hole in my side. The giant now fell to the ground and died. But I, too, was weak, and my life's blood was flowing out from my side. But as I was thinking of closing my eyes for ever, the young maiden came running down the cellar steps. When I saw her I got up on my elbow and called out to her.

' "Run as quickly as you can and get the giant's sword, that is hanging on the nail by his bed, and cut off his head."

'She ran off and came quickly back with the sword, and, as brave and as strong as any man, she raised it over her head with her two hands, and cut the head off the giant.

' "Now," said I to her, "I'll die easy."

' "You'll not die at all,' said she, 'for I'll carry you to the giant's cauldron of cure, and it will heal all your wounds, and you'll be as well as ever."

'And there and then she raised me on her back and hurried off with me to another cellar where the cauldron of cure was kept. She raised me up to the edge to lower me into the cauldron, and as she did so the sight was leaving my eyes, and the death-faint was spreading over my brain. She lowered me into the healing water slowly and gently and no sooner did water touch my skin than I was in my health and strength again.

'Wasn't I near death at that second?' asked the Black Thief of King Conal.

'Indeed you were,' said the king, 'and even if you were not, I wouldn't put you into the pot, but I would give you your life, like the others, because only for you I myself wouldn't be here today, for I was that child that was to be made into the pie for the giant's supper.' And the king held up his left finger for all to see it was missing a joint.

'My father knew that it was the Black Thief who saved my life,' said the king, 'and he searched the wide world for you to give you a reward, but he never found you. So a hundred thousand welcomes before you, and now I will have a great feast prepared in your honour.'

So the feast went ahead, and when it was all over the king loaded the Black Thief with gold and silver, and rewards of every kind, and he gave the three steeds to the sons of the King of Erin to take back to show to their stepmother.

'When she has ridden around the kingdom with them,' said the king, 'let the horses go, and they will come back to me without fail.'

So the three brothers brought King Conal's steeds back to Erin, and they went to their stepmother, who had been on top of the castle ever since they left, watching for their return.

'You brought back the horses,' said the stepmother.

'We did,' said the brothers, 'but we are not bound to give them to you; your sentence was that we were to go for the horses of King Conal and bring them back here. We have done that.'

And with that they turned the horses around and let them go. Off went the steeds like the wind back to King Conal.

'May I go down into the castle now?' asked the stepmother.

'Not yet,' said the youngest, 'for I did not pass any sentence on you before we left for the game I won from you.'

'And what is your sentence?' asked the angry Queen.

'You are to stay where you are until you find three other sons of a king to go for King Conal's horses.'

When she heard this sentence, she dropped dead from the castle.

The Snow Maiden

A Russian folk-tale
retold by A. N. Afanasiev
translated and adapted by Stephen Corrin

Once upon a time in a tiny Russian village there lived an old man and his wife. They led a quiet, peaceful sort of life and would have been quite content but for one thing – they had no children to cheer them up.

One day in the middle of winter, when the snow was piled high in drifts along the village street, the old couple were standing by their window watching the children merrily dashing about in the snow, throwing snowballs, making snowmen, and having all sorts of fun and games. They felt very sad that none of the children out there was theirs.

'I'll tell you what,' said the old man suddenly. 'How about us two going outside and making a little snow-girl.'

'Yes, let's do that,' said his wife. So they put on their fur hats and their heavy winter coats and went round to the back of their hut, because they didn't want anybody to see them. There they began to mould the figure of a young girl out of the pure white snow. They started by piling up the snow into a great big ball. Then they skimmed enough of it off to give it the shape and size of a human body. Next they fitted on the arms and legs and stood it up. Finally they put on the neck and head. The old woman moulded a delicate little nose and carefully outlined a pair of lips. The old man drew the eyes and no sooner had he finished than the lips became ruby red, the face took on a natural colour and the eyes themselves became alive and alert. The couple stared in astonishment: the snow girl was smiling at them. She pulled herself away from where they had planted her and stood before them – a living creature! She shook her head

prettily and the snow fell away, showing tresses of golden hair. She was real! She was alive! And what a delight she was to look at! The old couple were overjoyed. They could not stop admiring her.

Hour by hour, day by day, the Snow Maiden grew more beautiful. Her lovely skin remained white as snow but her golden hair grew down to her waist.

And as she grew she became like a daughter to the old couple. She did all the work in the little hut, and when the work was done she would sing, and all the villagers would stop to listen. The old couple simply doted on her, she was so kind and modest.

Winter passed and the spring sun spread its warmth everywhere. Fresh green grass replaced the winter snow and the song of the woodlarks brightened everyone's heart. But the Snow Maiden seemed to change; she grew sad.

'What ails you, daughter?' they asked her. 'You've been so happy all the winter. What is the matter now?'

'Nothing is the matter, Father. I am very well, Mother,' replied the Snow Maiden.

By now there was no trace of the winter snow, the flowers were blooming, the fields and meadows were joyous with colour and the cheerful twittering of birds could be heard everywhere. But the Snow Maiden, from day to day, grew quieter and sadder. She avoided the sun. She would brighten up if she could find a little shade and a cool corner and the rain, too, was welcome to her. Once, during a hailstorm, she got quite excited and tried to catch the hailstones as though they were precious stones. But when the sun shone through again and the hailstones melted away, she wept bitterly, just like a sister mourning for her departed brother.

Spring went quickly by, followed by a warm summer. All the girls in the village met together in the woods, singing and dancing and getting ready to go gathering berries.

'Come with us, Snow Maiden,' they called to her. 'Come and join our summer dance.'

But the Snow Maiden showed no wish at all to go with them. She drew back into the shadows and would not listen when her old mother pleaded with her, 'Come, daughter, go and make merry with your friends!'

The girls, laughing and singing, took no notice of her unwillingness and pulled her along. The Snow Maiden dragged her feet and looked down, full of sadness. The girls picked flowers, wove garlands, sang songs and danced in a ring, but the Snow Maiden stood alone, all by herself, as before, looking sadly down at the ground.

As the shadows lengthened towards evening the girls started to gather brushwood for a camp fire. And when it was burning nicely they took turns jumping over it. But the Snow Maiden kept her distance until, when her turn came, the girls came and pushed her gently towards the warming flames. She jumped over the fire and suddenly . . . melted quickly away, leaving only a floating white mist. The girls went looking for her but they never found her. The only reply to their calls was the echo of their voices in the woods.

The old woman's sorrow was deep indeed when the Snow Maiden did not return.

'It is my fault,' she said. 'I should not have persuaded her to go with the others.'

But her husband comforted her. 'Don't be downcast, my dear,' he said. 'After all, she was a child of the snow and did not feel at home when the warm weather came. Deep in my old bones I feel she will come back again, as surely as spring follows winter and winter follows autumn.'

'Yes, perhaps she will,' said the old woman. And so they enjoyed the summer, hoping that winter would bring their daughter back again.

The Clever Peasant Girl

a Czech tale
retold by Marie Burg

Once upon a time there were two brothers, one of them a wealthy farmer without children and the other a poor peasant with a daughter called Manka. When the girl was twelve years old he sent her to his wealthy brother to work as a goose girl. For two years she worked for her keep and after that time her uncle employed her as a maid.

'Listen, Manka,' he said to her one day. 'Instead of your wages I'll give you a calf two weeks old. I'll bring it up for you and it'll be more use to you than money.'

'Yes, let's do that,' Manka replied. From that time on she worked harder than ever before and never cost her uncle a penny. But her uncle was a rogue. For three years Manka served him faithfully, but then her father fell ill and she had to return home. Before leaving she asked her uncle for the calf, which had grown into a good cow.

He made all sorts of excuses, saying that he had never promised anything, that he could not possibly give her something as valuable as a cow, and tried to palm the girl off with a paltry sum of money. But she was by no means satisfied with such a poor bagain. She returned home in tears and told her father what had happened.

As soon as her father was well again he went to the nearby town and brought the matter before the Judge. After asking many questions, the Judge sent for the wealthy brother, who knew that he would have to part with his cow, unless he succeeded in winning the Judge over to his side. The Judge did not quite know what to do for the best: the poor man was in the right, yet he did not want to make the rich man angry.

So the Judge solved the problem in a cunning way. He spoke to each of the brothers separately, and he gave each of them a riddle to solve: 'What is sharpest, what is sweetest, what is richest?'

Whoever found the right answer first would have the cow.

The two brothers went on their way home, both of them in a pretty bad temper and puzzled about the riddle.

'Well, what happened?' asked the wife of the rich farmer when her husband returned home.

'I'm in a fine mess,' he said, adding a few rude remarks about the Judge.

'What's the matter? You didn't lose your case, or did you?'

'Lose? No, I didn't lose it, and for all I know I may still win.'

Then he repeated the riddle the judge had asked him to solve.

'What a childish riddle! I know all the answers. What could be sharper than our black dog? What could be sweeter than our honey? What could be richer than our money-box?'

'Wife, you are right. You've found the answers and the cow will be ours.'

With these words the man sat down and enjoyed the good meal his wife had prepared for him.

The poor peasant was rather sad when he returned home to his wife and daughter.

'Well, Dad, how did it go?' Manka wanted to know.

He told her about the riddle.

'Nothing worse than that? Cheer up, Dad, I'll soon find the answers. Just wait till tomorrow. I'll tell you all about it in the morning.'

All the same the poor farmer was so worried that he did not sleep a wink all night. In the morning Manka had her answers ready. 'Tell the Judge that sleep is the sweetest thing, that the eye is the sharpest, and the earth the richest. But don't tell him who told you.'

The father went back to the Judge, wondering if his answers would be the right ones.

The Judge first called the wealthy brother.

'I believe I know the answers,' the rich farmer said. 'For what could be sharper than my dog who hears everything? What could be sweeter than my honey that has been lying in a cask for four years? And what could be richer than the box in which I keep all my money?'

'My dear friend,' the Judge told him, shrugging his shoulders, 'I do not think that your answers are correct. Let me hear now what your brother has to say.'

'Sir, I believe that the sharpest thing is the eye that can see through everything. The sweetest thing is sleep, for sleep can make you forget your worries and give you happy dreams on top of it. And surely the richest thing must be the earth from which all wealth comes.'

'You guessed correctly and you shall have the cow. But tell me who it was who told you the answers, for I do not believe that you could find out for yourself.'

At first the peasant did not want to admit the truth, but, when the Judge insisted, he owned that his daughter had helped him.

'Well, if your daughter is as clever as that, tell her to come and see me tomorrow. But she must come neither dressed nor undressed, neither by day nor by night, neither on foot nor in a carriage.'

Now the poor man was worried again.

'My dear girl,' he said to Manka on entering the cottage, 'you guessed right. But the Judge simply would not believe that the answers came out of my head, so I had to tell him that you helped me. Now he wants you to come to him yourself. But you must be neither dressed nor undressed, you must go neither by day nor by night, and you must travel neither on foot nor in a carriage.'

'Don't worry, Dad. I'll manage all right.'

Two hours after midnight Manka got up. She dressed quickly, putting on nothing but a thin sack. On one foot she was wearing a shoe but no stocking, on the other a stocking but no shoe. When the clock struck three – at the very moment when night is about to change into day – she rode to town on her goat.

The Judge was waiting for her. Looking out of his window, he could see for himself how cleverly the girl had solved the tricky problem. He went up to her, saying, 'What a clever girl you are. If it suits you I will take you for my wife.'

'Why not?' Manka replied casually. 'It would suit me very well.'

The bridegroom took the arm of his clever and pretty bride and led her into his house. Then he sent for her father and for the tailor who was to make new clothes for Manka, for she needed clothes that would be suitable for the wife of a Judge.

The day before the wedding the Judge asked his wife-to-be never to meddle in his affairs. That was something he would never stand for. Should she try to interfere in what he considered to be his affairs, she would be sent back to her father.

'I'll do just as you wish,' Manka promised.

The following day the wedding took place. Manka became a lady of importance. She soon got used to her new position, she was kind to everyone, and people liked her very much.

One day two peasants came to the Judge. One of them was leading a foal. They wanted the Judge to decide which of them was to own the animal. The peasant who owned the mare claimed the foal and the man who owned the stallion also insisted it should be his.

The owner of the stallion was wealthy and important. After he had talked to the Judge alone, the latter decided in his favour.

But the wife of the Judge had overheard the conversation and disliked the unfair way in which her husband had acted. She decided to take matters into her own hands. She approached the farmer who had lost his foal as he was about to leave the house. 'Why do you allow the Judge to cheat you like that? The foal should go to the man who owns the mare.'

'I too think I've been cheated. But what can a simple man like myself do against the Judge?'

'Leave it to me. If you promise not to give me away I'll give you a sound piece of advice. Tomorrow about noon you must climb the top of Skarman Hill and pretend to be fishing. About that time my husband will be passing by with some of his friends. When he sees you he is sure to ask what you're doing. You must reply with these words: "If a stallion can have a foal, fish can swim on top of a hill." '

The man thanked Manka and promised to do as she suggested.

The following day towards noon he could be seen climbing Skarman Hill and throwing out fishing nets from the top of the hill. The Judge, hunting with his friends, soon passed by. He stopped and inquired what the peasant was doing.

'I'm fishing,' was the reply.

'Are you mad?' cried the Judge. 'Have you ever heard of fish swimming on top of a hill?'

'If a stallion can have a foal, fish can swim on top of a hill.'

The Judge turned red as a peony. He beckoned to the peasant to step aside so that he could talk to him without being overheard by his friends.

'All right,' he said, 'that foal is yours. But you must tell me one thing – who gave you the idea to answer as you did?'

At first the peasant did not want to tell the truth, yet in the end the Judge found out that it was his own wife who had helped the man.

On his return home the Judge did not even look at his wife, let alone speak to her. She guessed what was wrong and waited to see what would happen.

After some time her husband, thoroughly angry, asked her, 'Do you remember what you promised the day before we got married?'

'I do.'

'Why then did you interfere in my affairs? Why did you side with the peasant against your husband? Why?'

'Because I hate injustice. The poor farmer had been cheated, and you know it.'

'This is none of your business. Now go back where you came from. However, I do not want you to think that I am unfair to you, therefore you may take with you whatever you value most.'

'Thank you for all your kindness. If you cannot forgive me I will do as you say and return to my father. But let's have one more meal together before we part. Let's be happy together and behave as if nothing had happened.'

Quickly Manka went into the kitchen and ordered a good dinner and some of the best wine.

When dinner was served, husband and wife ate and drank a good deal. Manka encouraged the Judge to drink several glasses of the strong wine. When she noticed that he was getting sleepy, she beckoned to the servant to bring a special glass of wine. Then she begged the Judge to drink to her health.

Soon he was fast asleep. Without losing any time Manka ordered the servants to put her husband to bed. Then they picked him up – bed and all – and carried him out of the house to the cottage where Manka's father lived. They arrived at midnight and, after she had explained to her father what had happened, he made them welcome.

The sun stood high in the sky when at last the Judge woke up. He looked round and rubbed his eyes, for he was amazed to find himself in a room he did not know. After a while his wife entered the room. She was dressed in the wide red skirt and the little white bonnet Czech peasant women used to wear.

'Are you still here?' he asked.

'Why shouldn't I be here? I'm at home, after all.'

'Why then am I here?'

'Didn't you allow me to take with me what I valued most? Well, it's you I value most. So I've taken you with me.'

Laughing, the Judge said, 'I forgive you, for I see that you are cleverer than I am. From now on you shall be Judge instead of me.'

And so it was. Manka agreed, and ever since she took over the work of her husband all has been well with the people in their district.

Volkh's Journey to the East

a Russian tale
retold by E. M. Almedingen

About two miles to the east of Kiev in a small timbered house by the shore of a lake lived a widowed gentlewoman called Martha and her only son, Volkh.

Martha was poor, and she could not afford to buy any of those things which were enjoyed by boys of Volkh's age – green leather boots, coats of scarlet cloth, a sable cap, a horse, and a really good bow. Volkh ran barefoot, he wore rough smocks in the summer and sheepskins in the winter, had a bow made of withies, and rode a shaggy little pony which was as stubborn as a donkey.

Volkh did not know that his mother had a rare jewel hidden away in the chest in the back room of the house. It was an emerald buckle given to Martha on her wedding-day by her godmother, a wise old woman.

'There is great virtue in the buckle,' she had said then. 'It is neither for wearing nor for selling. Keep it hidden until the day when someone asks for it, and it will cost you dear to part with it, but you must do so.'

'How can anyone ask for it when nobody will ever know I have got it, and why should I have to give it up?' Martha had asked, but the old woman would not tell her, and soon after she died.

Now Volkh, who could not remember his father, grumbled often enough about the poor way they lived. He longed for a smart scarlet coat and a bow made of good Norwegian yew. He grumbled about the wooden trenchers and cups they used at table. He sometimes longed for roast goose and sturgeon for dinner, and Martha could not always afford enough money for the porridge. And many a time she secretly wished that she might take the emerald buckle to Kiev, sell it to some foreign merchant, and come home, laden with many things for her son's enjoyment, but she dared not break her godmother's wish.

So Volkh passed his twelfth birthday. He had good skill with his bow, and, being of noble birth, he could be sent to Kiev to join the Prince's household, but Martha knew that she could never afford to equip him for such service. She did not quite know what future awaited him, and she tried not to worry too much. In spite of all his frequent bouts of discontent, Volkh was a good son, and on many occasions Martha was proud of his courage. Volkh was not afraid to wander off into the neighbouring woods, and he always came back with something for the larder in his pouch, and he was very clever with his fishing rods.

One summer morning Martha was combing her hair by the window when she heard a great noise outside the gate. Her first thought was that Volkh, who had gone out at dawn, had been killed by a bear. Martha hid her hair under a linen coif and ran down the carved wooden stairway as fast as her trembling legs would carry her.

At once she breathed in deep relief. Her son stood there, his wet smock gloving his body, his hair, legs and arms all covered with weeds, and by the side of him was an elderly man, dripping from head to foot, his pilgrim's cloak torn and muddy. There was a small crowd behind him – all shouting and clapping. The old pilgrim had fallen into the lake and Volkh had jumped in and pulled him out.

When things were somewhat quieter, Martha told her maid to get some dry clothing and to set the table for a meal. She offered broiled fish and a rye loaf with apologies for such a scant breakfast, but the old pilgrim said courteously:

'Madam, I am not used to rich fare.'

When they had eaten, Volkh ran away to look for the fishing-rod he had mislaid, and the pilgrim said:

'Madam, you are known to me though I am a stranger to you. When I was in Jerusalem I had a command given me to come and see you on my return to Rus.'

'Who gave it to you?' asked Martha quickly, but the old man did not answer the question and went on:

'You had an emerald buckle given to you on your wedding-day and I am here to ask for it.'

Martha said sadly:

'This is a very poor manor, and I had always hoped that nobody would come for the buckle whilst I was alive so that my son might have something for his future,' and she sighed, tears welling up in her eyes.

'Your son will never lack for anything,' the pilgrim said gently, but Martha shook her head. She thought that the old man would probably offer the buckle at some shrine along his way. It certainly seemed unfair, but there was nothing to be done. She got up and went into the back room and returned, a small lime-wood box in her hands.

'I'd much rather not look at it again.' Martha laid the box on the table. 'May God's blessing be your companion all along the way.'

The pilgrim bowed and hid the box in the folds of his smock. Martha never watched him leave the room – her eyes were all misted with tears. She just did not know what she could do about Volkh's future. She never knew how long she had sat by the table when his excited voice roused her.

'Mother! Mother! Look! I have found it all by the lake shore and everything fits me.'

Martha raised her head and remained at gaze. Volkh stood there, a magnificent hauberk of Damascene mesh mail on him. He wore beautiful white linen breeches and green boots with silver tassels. There was a bright red plume on his helmet, and his hands, gloved in stout buff leather, held a short pike and an axe.

'Son,' Martha gasped at last. 'Am I awake or asleep? You look like a Knight of the Golden Table!'

'No, Mother, because there was no shield among the things,' Volkh replied.

'But who gave you these wonderful things?'

'The pilgrim. I saw him leave the house, make for the lake shore, and stand there some time, and then I saw the things appear one by one – so quickly, too, it seemed as though they came either from the air or from the ground. I ran as fast as I could. I thought it was all a dream. He waved his hand, said they were all for me, and vanished. Here is a piece of writing.'

Neither Martha nor Volkh knew their letters. They took the small piece of parchment to the parish clerk, who read out:

'Six wishes for Volkh. Three wishes for Prince Danilo. There is no tenth wish.'

'Why, that means that I must ride to Kiev at once,' cried Volkh, 'and ask the little Prince what his wishes are.'

'God protect you along the way,' said the parish clerk severely – he had not seen the pilgrim and rather doubted the story told him by Martha.

Mother and son returned homewards. She said:

'Volkh, I am afraid that it is a far distance for that old pony of yours, and some of the going is rough.'

'Oh, I wish I had a horse to take me to the very gates of Kiev within an instant,' cried the boy, and the very next instant he was in the saddle, a beautiful black horse under him, and he was no longer at the gate of his mother's house. There stood the great turreted walls of Kiev. Beyond, domes, cupolas and roofs blended into a marvellous tapestry of gold, crimson, blue and green. Yet no bells could be heard, and the watch at the gates were sobbing bitterly. Volkh leapt out of the saddle.

'Oh, what has happened?' he asked.

'It is our little Prince Danilo,' gulped one of the men. 'Yesterday he rode out with his falcon, and he had his body-guard, too, but he was kidnapped by an enemy from a very far country – they say they are all magicians there, and one of their men shot an arrow into the city with a message for the Prince. I cannot rightly tell you what was in it, but all the Knights of the Golden Table left Kiev within a few minutes. Not one of them has yet returned. Well, young sir, ride on into the city!'

Volkh had heard so much of the crowds, the markets, the

gaiety of life in Kiev. He found it a city of mourning. Nobody
was to be seen in the streets, and all the shops were closed and
the markets empty. The people crowded the Cathedral and all
the churches to pray for the rescue of their little Prince,
Vladimir's only son and heir. Volkh rode on to the gateway of
the palace. He knew well that he had the right to ask to see his
sovereign and now he understood why his knightly gear had
been given him. Volkh felt very excited and not a little scared.
He also remembered that he must be very careful about wish-
ing. He had already expressed a wish for a horse. Five wishes
only were left to him.

According to custom Volkh took off his helmet and belt when
he reached the porch of the palace. The captain of the men-at-
arms asked his name and added:

'Prince Vladimir will not refuse to see you, but have you some
really urgent business? He is in great distress.'

Volkh replied, his words a surprise to himself:

'I am here to ask for the Prince's blessing. I mean to rescue the
little Prince.'

The man stared very hard and pulled at his beard.

'Prince Vladimir is in no mood for such unkind jokes, boy.
You don't look old enough to carry a sword.'

'I am sorry. I had to leave it in the porch together with my
helmet and belt. I wish I had it on me to prove—' and Volkh
stopped because the belt, the sword dangling from it, was
round his waist in an instant.

'Four wishes left,' gasped Volkh. 'Really, I must be careful.'

The captain of the men-at-arms was shaking from head to
foot.

'Take it off, take it off at once, and tell it to stay where you put
it, and you are not to scare Prince Vladimir the way you scared
me.'

Presently Volkh was led into the crimson painted hall, and the
Prince received him kindly enough.

'Have you come to ask me to right some injustice, son?' he
asked.

'No, my lord,' Volkh replied. 'I have come for your blessing,' and he knelt, the tips of his fingers touching the edge of the golden table. 'I mean to ride and rescue the young Prince.'

Vladimir stared.

'You have no idea what you are talking about! He has been taken to a country called Persia – and they flew away with him. His bodyguard saw it happen. All Persians are great magicians, and the Shah of Persia has asked for a ransom – ten thousand white heifers without a blemish. All the Knights of the Golden Table have ridden to look for them. I doubt if they will find as many hundred,' and Prince Vladimir sat very still. He thought of his wife, Princess Eupraxia, weeping in her room upstairs.

'I have not got a single white heifer to offer, my lord,' said Volkh, 'but it is my duty to go,' and he told Vladimir about the pilgrim's visit, the miraculous gift of equipment and horse, and the little piece of parchment.

'It is my duty to go, my lord,' he said again, and Prince Vladimir raised his right hand.

'God bless you, my son, and He alone can protect you. The hazards are far more than you think.'

Volkh rose, bowed, and murmured:

'Oh, I wish I were in the saddle and at the place where the young Prince is!'

No sooner had he said it than he found himself in a strange mountainous country. He sat in the saddle, facing a cleft between two huge rocks. To the left of him stretched a valley with innumerable white tents. To the right of him, he saw four huge poles so tall that he could hardly see their tops where two criss-cross poles were joined together, and from the middle swung an enormous gilt cage – most sumptuously furnished with cushions and coverlets of white velvet and violet silk, and there sat little Prince Danilo dressed in a pink and green striped Persian robe, with a Persian cap on his head. The very sight of these clothes infuriated Volkh. How dared they put them on a prince of Kiev?

The child raised his head, and Volkh saw that he had been crying.

'I am from Kiev, Prince Danilo,' said Volkh and jumped out of

the saddle. 'I have come to take you home.'

The little Prince stood up and clung to the bars.

'You mustn't come too near,' he said. 'A kindly Persian woman tried to give me some food, and two huge hounds ran from behind a rock as soon as she touched the bars, and they killed her.'

Volkh unsheathed his sword.

'I expect I could deal with those hounds, Prince Danilo, but before I get any nearer, please tell me how the cage opens. The bars go all the way round and there doesn't seem to be a lock anywhere.'

'They welded the bars together,' sobbed the little Prince. 'They said my dear father would never get ten thousand white heifers for my ransom and that I would never come out. Oh dear, I am so hungry and thirsty, too!'

'Keep in good heart, Prince Danilo.' Volkh rode nearer and stretched out his hands towards the bars. At once two enormous hounds, fangs bared, sprang from behind a rock.

'I wish both of you were dead within an instant,' cried Volkh, and down they went at once.

'I have just three wishes left,' he thought, 'that is – three for myself. Wasn't there something about three wishes for Prince Danilo? I must find out,' and he said aloud: 'Well, one hurdle is behind us, and don't worry – I mean to get you out, but don't you wish you could have some food before the journey home?'

'Food?' echoed the little Prince. 'I wish I had a stale crust to chew!'

Volkh watched narrowly, but no stale crust appeared on the white velvet cushions.

'The spell must work differently for the little Prince,' he thought. 'And I have three wishes of my own left now. One for the cage to open, one for some food, and the third for the speedy return to Kiev. Now then,' Volkh took a deep breath and said: 'I wish the cage would open,' and at once the bars fell apart and the little Prince jumped down, right into Volkh's arms.

'Steady, Prince,' said Volkh. 'Now you must not ride hungry,' and again he spoke the words, and there was a table covered with a white cloth and laden with dishes; fragrant sturgeon soup, mushroom pies, roast fowl, honeybread and milk in a silver jug, and Prince Danilo urged Volkh to share all the good things with him. When they had eaten, Volkh said:

'Now for home,' and he was just about to lift the little Prince into the saddle when Danilo said sadly:

'These dreadful outlandish clothes! My father's people would think I had turned Persian! Oh for my little blue coat and my green boots with tassels!'

'Yes,' Volkh nodded sympathetically, 'I wish I could bring you home in those clothes,' and there stood the Prince in his blue coat and white shirt, its collar worked in red cross-stitch, and the high green boots.

'You are a very good magician.' The child clapped his hands for pleasure, but Volkh's face had gone white. He had spent the last wish.

'I suppose we had better hurry,' said the boy, and Volkh lifted him into the saddle.

Volkh's heart was beating wildly. If he turned the horse south, he would ride straight in the Persian camp. If he rode north, he might lose his way in the mountains. How far were they from Kiev? He could not tell, but he felt sure it was a fearful distance.

'Has your horse gone lame?' Prince Danilo asked politely, turned his head, and screamed. 'Look, they are going to chase us –'

It was true. Volkh spurred the horse and plunged into the rocky pass. He had spent his last wish, but at least he had a wonderful mount to ride, and the black horse flew like an eagle. Soon their pursuers were left far behind, but Volkh's horse was still galloping through the wild rocky country. For all Volkh knew, they were going farther and farther from Kiev, and he knew the sun was about to set. What could he do? The little paper mentioned three wishes for Prince Danilo, but the boy asked for food, and no food had come . . .

He reined in the horse on a narrow rocky shelf, and dismounted. Suddenly he felt so tired that he would have given all he had for an hour's sleep. The little Prince, still in the saddle, looked down and said softly:

'I suppose we are still far away from Kiev. I wish you were not so tired,' and no sooner had the child spoken than Volkh felt his fatigue slipping away. In fact, he thought he would have enough strength to cleave a rock in two. So here lay the key: the little Prince's wishes worked so long as they did not concern himself. And there were only two of them left. Volkh caught his breath.

'Well, we have ridden a good distance, and we cannot be very far away from Kiev –'

And he was about to mount when Danilo bent down and touched his shoulders.

'Oh, I wish you would not look so sad!'

And instantly Volkh was feeling as happy as he had never felt before – just when there was nothing for him to feel happy about. Then he had an idea, and he staked Danilo's last wish on it. If it failed, they were lost, 'and we must not fail,' thought Volkh stubbornly.

So he leapt into the saddle and said:

'I am sorry, Prince Danilo. I was thinking of my mother. She did not know that I would be coming here. She expected me home quite soon,' and having said it, Volkh prayed with all his might that the little Prince would answer in the right way.

Danilo said nothing for a moment. Then he whispered:

'Yes, I understand. I wish your mother could see you riding through the streets of Kiev!'

At once the grim rocks were gone. They were riding very slowly down the street of Wisdom, and Volkh's eyes caught Martha's happy proud face as she stood at the edge of the square. They rode on to the sound of bells and deafening cheers. Vladimir and Eupraxia rushed past the guard to greet them.

A little later Volkh and Martha were summoned into the crimson hall. All the Knights were still away looking for the white heifers for the Prince's ransom, but another oaken chair had been added to the others, and a small red-plumed helmet lay on the table in token of a Knight's presence in the palace. Martha burst into tears of joy, but Volkh stammered that he was not fit to be a Knight.

'But that is for your sovereign to say,' Vladimir told him and, bending forward, touched the boy's right shoulder.

The Living Kuan-Yin

a Chinese tale
retold by C. Kendall

Even though the family name of Chin means *gold*, it does not signify that everyone of that name is rich. Long ago, in the province of Chekiang, however, there was a certain wealthy Chin family of whom it was popularly said that its fortune was as great as its name. It seemed quite fitting, then, when a son was born to the family, that he should be called Po-wan, 'Million', for he was certain to be worth a million pieces of gold when he came of age.

With such a happy circumstance of names, Po-wan himself never doubted that he would have a never-ending supply of money chinking through his fingers, and he spent it accordingly – not on himself, but on any unfortunate who came to his attention. He had a deep sense of compassion for anyone in distress of body or spirit: a poor man had only to hold out his hand, and Po-wan poured gold into it; if a destitute widow and her brood of starvelings but lifted sorrowful eyes to his, he provided them with food and lodging and friendship for the rest of their days.

In such wise did he live that even a million gold pieces were not enough to support him. His resources so dwindled that finally he scarcely had enough food for himself; his clothes flapped threadbare on his wasted frame; and the cold seeped into his bone marrow for lack of a fire. Still he gave away the little money that came to him.

One day, as he scraped out half of his bowl of rice for a beggar even hungrier than he, he began to ponder on his destitute state.

'Why am I so poor?' he wondered. 'I have never spent extravagantly. I have never, from the day of my birth, done an evil deed. Why then am I, whose very name is A Million Pieces of Gold, no longer able to find even a copper to give this unfortunate creature, and have only a bowl of rice to share with him?'

He thought long about his situation and at last determined to go without delay to the South Sea. Therein, it was told, dwelt the all-merciful goddess, the Living Kuan-yin, who could tell the past and future. He would put his question to her and she would tell him the answer.

Soon he had left his home country behind and travelled for many weeks in unfamiliar lands. One day he found his way barred by a wide and furiously flowing river. As he stood first on one foot and then on the other, wondering how he could possibly get across, he heard a commanding voice calling from the top of an overhanging cliff.

'Chin Po-wan!' the voice said, 'if you are going to the South Sea, please ask the Living Kuan-yin a question for me!'

'Yes, yes, of course,' Po-wan agreed at once, for he had never in his life refused a request made of him. In any case, the Living Kuan-yin permitted each person who approached her three questions, and he had but one of his own to ask.

Craning his head towards the voice coming from above, he suddenly began to tremble, for the speaker was a gigantic snake with a body as large as a temple column. Po-wan was glad he had agreed so readily to the request.

'Ask her then,' said the snake, 'why I am not yet a dragon

even though I have practised self-denial for more than one thousand years?'

'That I will do, and gl-gladly,' stammered Po-wan, hoping that the snake would continue to practise self-denial just a bit longer. 'But, your . . . your Snakery . . . or your Serpentry, perhaps I should say . . . that is . . . you see, don't you . . . first I must cross this raging river, and I know not how.'

'That is no problem at all,' said the snake. 'I shall carry you across, of course.'

'Of course,' Po-wan echoed weakly. Overcoming his fear and his reluctance to touch the slippery-slithery scales, Chin Po-wan climbed on to the snake's back and rode across quite safely. Politely, and just a bit hurriedly, he thanked the self-denying serpent and bade him goodbye. Then he continued on his way to the South Sea.

By noon he was very hungry. Fortunately a nearby inn offered meals at a price he could afford. While waiting for his bowl of rice, he chatted with the innkeeper and told him of the Snake of the Cliff, which the innkeeper knew well and respected, for the serpent always denied bandits the crossing of the river. Inadvertently, during the exchange of stories, Po-wan revealed the purpose of his journey.

'Why then,' cried the innkeeper, 'let me prevail upon your generosity to ask a word for me.' He laid an appealing hand on Po-wan's ragged sleeve. 'I have a beautiful daughter,' he said, 'wonderfully amiable and pleasing of disposition. But although she is in her twentieth year, she has never in all her life uttered a single word. I should be very much obliged if you would ask the Living Kuan-yin why she is unable to speak.'

Po-wan, much moved by the innkeeper's plea for his mute daughter, of course promised to do so. For after all, the Living Kuan-yin allowed each person three questions and he had but one of his own to ask.

Nightfall found him far from any inn, but there were houses in the neighbourhood, and he asked for lodging at the largest. The owner, a man obviously of great wealth, was pleased to offer him a bed in a fine chamber, but first begged him to partake of a hot meal and good drink. Po-wan ate well, slept soundly, and, much refreshed, was about to depart the following morning, when his good host, having learned that Po-wan was journeying to the South Sea, asked if he would be kind enough to put a question for him to the Living Kuan-yin.

'For twenty years,' he said, 'from the time this house was built, my garden has been cultivated with the utmost care, yet in all those years, not one tree, not one small plant, has bloomed or borne fruit, and because of this, no bird comes to sing nor bee to gather nectar. I don't like to put you to a bother, Chin Po-wan, but as you are going to the South Sea anyway, perhaps you would not mind seeking out the Living Kuan-yin and asking her why the plants in my garden don't bloom?'

'I shall be delighted to put the question to her,' said Po-wan. For after all, the Living Kuan-yin allowed each person three questions, and he had but . . .

Travelling onward, Po-wan examined the quandary in which he found himself. The Living Kuan-yin allowed but three questions, and he had somehow, without quite knowing how, accumulated four questions. One of them would have to go unasked, but which? If he left out his own question, his whole journey would have been in vain. If, on the other hand, he left out the question of the snake, or the innkeeper, or the kind host, he would break his promise and betray their faith in him.

'A promise should never be made if it cannot be kept,' he told himself. 'I made the promises and therefore I must keep them. Besides, the journey will not be in vain, for at least some of these problems will be solved by the Living Kuan-yin. Furthermore, assisting others must certainly be counted as a good deed, and the more good deeds abroad in the land, the better for everyone, including me.'

At last he came into the presence of the Living Kuan-yin.

First, he asked the serpent's question. 'Why is the Snake of the Cliff not yet a dragon, although he has practised self-denial for more than one thousand years?'

And the Kuan-yin answered: 'On his head are seven bright pearls. If he removes six of them, he can become a dragon.'

Next, Po-wan asked the innkeeper's question: 'Why is the innkeeper's daughter unable to speak, although she is in the twentieth year of her life?'

And the Living Kuan-yin answered: 'It is her fate to remain mute until she sees the man destined to be her husband.'

Last, Po-wan asked the kind host's question: 'Why are there no blossoms in the rich man's garden, although it has been carefully cultivated for twenty years?'

And the Living Kuan-yin answered: 'Buried in the garden are seven big jars filled with silver and gold. The flowers will bloom if the owner will rid himself of half of the treasure.'

Then Chin Po-wan thanked the Living Kuan-yin and bade her good-bye.

On his return journey, he stopped first at the rich man's house to give him the Living Kuan-yin's answer. In gratitude the rich man gave him half the buried treasure.

Next Po-wan went to the inn. As he approached, the innkeeper's daughter saw him from the window and called out, 'Chin Po-wan! Back already! What did the Living Kuan-yin say?'

Upon hearing his daughter speak at long last, the joyful innkeeper gave her in marriage to Chin Po-wan.

Lastly, Po-wan went to the cliffs by the furiously flowing river

to tell the snake what the Living Kuan-yin had said. The grateful snake immediately give him six of the bright pearls and promptly turned into a magnificent dragon, the remaining pearl in his forehead lighting the headland like a great beacon.

And so it was that Chin Po-wan, that generous and good man, was once more worth a million pieces of gold.

Chura and Marwe

an African tale
retold by Humphrey Harman

Far to the east there is a great mountain, whose top is lacquered
with silver every month of the year. Upon the slopes of this once
lived a boy and a girl. He was called Chura and she Marwe and
they were slave children, got cheap and kept by a household of
the Chagga people to watch crops and herd goats.

Now Chura had a face like a toad's and Marwe was so beautiful that when people saw them together they exclaimed, 'Eh!
How is it that God could make two so different?'

That, however, was not how Marwe saw it. Chura was her
companion and the only one she had. They loved each other
dearly, were happy together and only when they were together,
for they had little else to be happy about.

One day they were sent to watch a field and keep the monkeys from eating the beans. The place was on the lower slopes of
the mountain, a clearing in the forest, and there all day the
children sat beating a pot with a stick whenever they heard a
monkey chatter thievishly behind the wall of leaves. Hemmed
in with tall trees, the field was airless and hot, and by late
afternoon they could stand their thirst no longer. They slipped
off to where a stream, cold from the snows above, fell noisily
down a cliff into a pool. The water there was deep and upon its
dark surface one leaf floated in a circle all day.

Here they drank hastily, washed the tiredness from their
faces, then ran back to the field. Alas; in the little time they had
been away the monkeys had stripped it.

Marwe wept and Chura stared at the plundered bean plants
with a bleak face. The folk they worked for were harsh and the

children knew they would be beaten. Chura tried to comfort his friend, but there was little of that he could give her and at last, in despair, she ran into the forest. Chura followed, calling for her to stop, and was just in time to see her throw herself into the pool where, at once, she sank from sight.

Chura could not swim and he knew the pool to be deep. He ran round the edge calling, but it was no use. The dark water quietened, the leaf again circled placidly and Marwe was gone.

Chura went back to the household and told those who owned him of the loss of Marwe and the crop. They followed him to the pool, where nothing was to be seen, and then to the field, where the sight of ruined plants made them angry. They beat Chura, and some days later, grieving for Marwe and tired of ill-treatment, he ran away and the Chagga never saw him again.

Soon another pair of children watched the crops or herded goats, and whether they found life better than Chura and Marwe had is unknown.

When Marwe flung herself into the pool she sank slowly through water which changed from bright light of noon to the deep blue of late evening and finally to the darkness of a night with neither moon nor stars. And there she stepped out into the Underworld, shook water from her hair and wandered, chilled to the heart by the greyness of the place.

Presently she came to a hut on the slope of a hill, with an old woman outside preparing supper for the small children playing on the swept earth at her feet. Beyond the hut, just where the hill curved over and away, was a village that seemed as if it had just been built, for the logs of the stockade were white as if the bark had been stripped from them that day and the thatch of the houses was new-dried and trim.

The old woman asked Marwe where she was going, and Marwe replied timidly that she was a stranger and alone and wanted to go to the village she saw above, to ask for food and perhaps work so that she could live her life.

'It's not yet time to go there,' said the woman. 'Stay with me

and work here. You'll not go hungry or lack a place by the fire if
you do so.'

So Marwe accepted this offer and lived with the old woman.
She cared for the children, fetched water from the stream and
weeded a garden. Her new mistress was kind and so life for
Marwe went on without hardship.

Only sometimes she pined for the sunlight and bird-song of
the world above, for here it was never anything but grey. And
always she longed for Chura.

And now let us follow what happened to him.

He drifted from village to village of the Chagga, asking for food and work but, because of his ugliness, no one would take him in. Food they offered hastily and then they told him uneasily to go. It seemed to men and even more to women that such an ill-favoured face must have been earned by great evil and could only bring with it worse luck. So, wandering from hamlet to village, gradually inching his way round the mountain, he was fed by unwilling charity or, more often, by what small game he could kill or field he could rob. As the years passed he grew strong and hard but no better looking.

One day he left the forest and the tall grass of the foothills and walked north into the sun-bitten plain. Here the trees were bleached and shrunken, standing wide apart, their thin leaves throwing little shade. Between them the ants built red towers and covered every dead leaf or stick with a crust of dry earth.

A juiceless land where grass was scarce and water more so, and here lived the Masai.

They are a people who greatly love three things, children, cattle and war. Standing like storks upon one leg, holding spears with blades long as an arm, and shields blazing with colour, they guarded their cattle and looked with amused indifference upon the lives of other men.

They found Chura wandering and thirsty, carelessly decided not to kill him, made him a servant. At his ugliness they only laughed.

'What's it to us if you look like a toad?' they shouted. 'All men other than Masai are animals anyway. And usually look like them.'

So Chura milked cows, mended cattle fences and made himself useful until one night a lion attacked the calves. Then he took a spear from a hut and went out and killed it.

'Wah!' said the Masai when they came running and found Chura with the great beast dead at his feet. 'Alone and without a shield! This is a new light you show yourself in. Well, you weren't born Masai, though plainly some mistake's been made by the gods over that. Somewhere within you there must be a

Masai of sorts, otherwise you couldn't have done this. We'll accept you for one.'

So they gave him the spear he had borrowed, and a shield whose weight made him stagger. When the lion's skin had been cured they made from it a headdress that framed Chura's face in a circle of long tawny hair and added two feet to his height.

'There, now you look almost human,' they said. 'Only something must be done about that name of yours. It means toad and no Masai could live with it.'

'Well then, what am I to be called?' asked Chura.

'Hm. Punda Malia (Donkey)?' suggested one.

'No, no, Kifaru (Rhino),' said another.

'What about Nguruwe (Pig)?' threw in another.

'If you can't be civil . . .' began Chura, taking a firm grip on his spear.

'Heh! Keep your temper, Brother. We mean no harm. Now, what can your name be . . .?'

They called for a pot of beer and spent a happy evening making suggestions and falling about with laughter at their own wit. But finally they pulled themselves together and found for Chura a name which seemed to them far more suitable than the one he had brought with him.

When Marwe had lived for a number of years in the Underworld and grown to be as beautiful a woman as she had been a child, she became homesick. The old woman noticed her sadness and asked what caused it. Marwe hesitated, because she did not want to seem ungrateful for the kindness that had been given to her but, in the end, she said that she pined to go back to her own world. The old woman was not offended.

'Ah,' she said, 'then it's time you went to the village. In this matter I can't help, but they may.'

Next day Marwe climbed the hill and waited at the village gate. When she had sat there for some time a number of old men came out. They were dressed in cotton robes that shone through the gloom about, and they greeted her and asked what she wanted. Marwe replied that she wished to return to the world above.

'Hm,' they said. 'We'll see, yes, we'll see.'

Then one who seemed the most important among them asked, 'Child, which would you sooner have, the warm or the cold?'

The question bewildered Marwe. 'I don't understand,' she replied.

Shadows seemed to cross their faces and their voices grew fainter. 'That's nothing to us,' they said. 'You've heard our question and we can do nothing unless you answer. Which would you prefer, the warm or the cold?'

Marwe understood that this was a test which it must be important for her to consider with care.

'Warmth . . . or cold?' she pondered. 'Well, everyone would sooner have warmth than cold because cold is bitter and difficult to endure, while warmth is life itself. Yet surely their riddle can't be as easy as that.'

When she had thought again, as deeply as she could, it seemed that if the choice was between what is usually thought to be good and bad, her life pointed the other way.

'For,' said she, 'Chura was ugly and unwanted, yet he was kind and I loved him. And the Underworld is feared by everyone, yet here I've met greater kindness than I ever knew in the sunlit world above.'

And she made up her mind and said, 'No matter what others believe, I'll trust my own wisdom and choose the cold.'

The old men listened to her answer with faces from which she could read nothing, and they offered her two pots. From the mouth of one rose steam, while the other sent out a chill that struck to the bone of a hand brought near it.

'Choose as you've chosen,' they urged her and so, faithful to her own belief, she dipped a hand into the cold pot and brought it out covered to the elbow with richly-made bracelets.

'Don't hesitate to take more,' they urged her. 'Neither we nor the pots will be offended.'

So she reached in her other arm and in turn both her feet, and

147

came out heavy with bangles and anklets, heavy precious things made from copper and gold, ornaments worth more than the tribute of a whole tribe.

The old men smiled and told her that she had chosen well and been wise. And still they loaded her with treasures, necklaces of shell, rings and ear-drops. They brought her a fine kilt worked all over with gold wire and beads that glowed blue as the skies she remembered from the world above.

'Now,' they said, 'we've one more gift: a piece of advice. When you are back in your own world you'll wish in time to marry and there'll be no shortage of those who'll ask for you. Go softly, don't hasten. Wait for someone with the name of Simba to ask, and choose him.'

Then, gathering their robes clear of their feet, the old ones led her to the pool. Gently they urged her in and she rose like a thought until she broke the sunlit surface, where the leaf still circled and birds sang in the trees about.

She left the water, sat upon the bank with the light dancing on her finery, and waited for the world to find her.

And very soon it did.

News spread that beside a pool in the forest sat a woman, rich and of amazing beauty, waiting for a husband. They flocked to her with offers, handsome young men, rich landowners, daring hunters, great warriors, even powerful chiefs. And all singing much the same tune, 'Here's fame or wealth or power or glory or beauty or . . . if only you'll marry me!'

She pointed at each one of them the same sharp little question, 'What's your name?'

'Name! Why, it's Nyati or Mamba or Tembo or Ndovu or . . .' and so on. No end of names and at all she shook her head and replied, 'I'm sorry, but that will not be the name of my husband.'

Now the news flew even as far as the plain , down where the cattle trudge through the dust, the lion hunts and the vulture sits upon the thorn. At last it reached Chura, and at once he took spear and shield and came tirelessly running and his heart singing, 'Marwe's back from the Underworld and I'll see her!'

When he came to where she sat beside her pool and cried
'Marwe!' she recognized his ugliness even framed as it was by a
lion's mane. Part of her laughed and the rest wept.

'Oh, Chura,' she cried. 'Why is life so unkind? I shall never
love anyone but you, yet my fate says that we can't marry.'

'Then who can you marry?' he demanded.

'Only a man named Simba.'

'But that's my name,' he roared. 'Simba! Lion! The Masai
named me that when I killed a lion.'

So, of course, they were married. What was there to stop
them? It would have been striking fate across the face not to
marry. But everyone marvelled that so beautiful a woman
should choose so ugly a husband.

They paid no attention to them and – it's a strange thing and
scarcely to be believed – but, do you know, the moment they

were married something happened to his ugly toad's face and he became good to look at.

Well, passable.

So they say.

I don't imagine for one moment that Marwe cared either way.

The Golden Candelabra

a Persian tale
retold by Anne Sinclair Mehdevi

There was a time and there wasn't a time in the long ago when a rich merchant lived in the city of Nishapour. He was a widower and lived alone, except for his daughter whose name was Pari. The merchant loved her more than anything in the world, and for this reason he kept her locked in his house in a velvet-lined room so that no harm could befall her.

Pari grew tall and graceful. Her hair was as black as a blackbird's wing and her eyes were like two sapphires. Her father gave her everything her heart desired – silken gowns and ivory chairs and a bed of ebony wood. When the weather was warm, she fanned herself with a fan of peacock feathers.

One day, Pari said to her father. 'Father, you have granted me every wish. Now that I am sixteen, I wish to go into the city like other people and see the world.'

'My child,' said the merchant, 'this wish shall also be granted. You are soon to be married to Golhak Khan, the tea merchant. I have arranged it for you. Then you will ride to his fine house in a carriage. Then you will see the world in all its ugliness and all its beauty.'

Golhak Khan was an old man with a red beard. He was a kind man, but Pari did not want to be married to him. That night, she lay upon her bed of ebony and wept.

The next day she said to her father, 'Father, you have granted me every wish. It is dark in my chamber. I wish for a golden candelabra that holds a hundred candles, so my chamber will be as bright as the great world outside.'

'You shall have your wish, my child,' said her father, and he

151

sent out messengers to find the finest goldsmith in Persia.

The goldsmith came from Isfahen, and, when Pari was alone with him, she said, 'If you make my golden candelabra exactly as I tell you, I shall give you my fan of peacock feathers and an ivory chair for your wife to sit in when she spins.'

'Speak, my lady, I shall obey,' said the goldsmith.

'And you must promise on the head of your wife that you will never tell my father the secret of the golden candelabra,' said Pari.

And, being a greedy fellow, he did not want to refuse the extra gifts. 'My lips are sealed,' he said. 'And besides, I shall be far away in Isfahan.'

So, Pari told him to fashion the candelabra in the shape of a date-palm tree with one hundred branches of beaten gold. Each branch held a candle that would burn for a week. And, in the trunk of the golden palm tree, the goldsmith made a secret door – as Pari told him to – so finely fitted that no one could tell it was there.

When the candelabra was finished, the goldsmith returned to Isfahan, and the candelabra was placed in Pari's chamber. One night, when her father was asleep, she took seven loaves of bread and a jug of goat's milk and went to the candelabra. She pressed the hidden jewel which opened the secret door, and she stepped inside the golden trunk. Then she closed the door after her.

The next morning, when her father came to greet her, he found her room empty. He was beside himself with grief. He sent messengers through the city offering rewards to anyone who could give him news of his beloved daughter. But Pari was nowhere to be found. After five days, the merchant went to a wise man. 'My daughter has vanished,' he said. 'What can I do to recover her?'

The wise man answered, 'The golden candelabra has brought misfortune to your house. Sell it, and your daughter will return to you.'

So, the merchant shipped the golden candelabra to Samarkand, where it was placed in a shop window for sale. The very next day, the Prince of Samarkand came riding by on his horse as he returned from hunting. When he saw the golden candelabra, he reined in his horse, and entered the shop himself and bought it. The candelabra was placed in the Prince's chamber near a window where he could see its glistening branches in the dawn light as he woke up.

Pari, who had been inside the trunk of the golden candelabra all this time, had finished her seven loaves of bread and had drunk her jug of goat's milk, and she was hungry. 'I must open the secret door and find something to eat or I shall never see the great world,' she said to herself. 'I wonder where I am?' She put her ear to the secret door and listened.

She heard voices, for the Prince was talking with his servant. So, Pari kept very still and waited, growing hungrier and hungrier. At last, the Prince, who was tired from his long day's hunting, fell asleep without eating his supper. The room was silent, and Pari noiselessly opened the secret door and stepped out.

She found herself in a chamber hung with rich damask and tiled with black marble. 'How beautiful the world is,' she thought as she looked around in delight.

She did not see the Prince, who was fast asleep inside the curtains of his bed, but she saw the Prince's supper laid out on a small table. She tiptoed across the room and ate up all his food. Then she returned to the golden candelabra, stepped inside, closed the secret door after her, and fell asleep.

Next morning, when the Prince awoke, he remembered that he had forgotten to eat his supper. He rose and went across the room to the table where his supper had been. Every plate was empty.

He called his servant. 'Did anyone enter my room in the night when I was asleep?' he asked.

'No, master,' said the servant. 'I have been on guard outside the door all night.'

The next night, the Prince again fell asleep after hunting without eating, and again Pari crept from the candelabra and ate his supper. This happened for three nights. On the fourth night,

the Prince decided to stay awake. He went to bed as usual, but he left the curtains of his bed partly open. At midnight, he heard a soft noise like the rustle of silk.

Suddenly, the trunk of the candelabra opened and Pari stepped out. She went across the room, sat down at the little table and began peeling an apple. The prince thought she was the most beautiful creature he had ever seen, and his heart was heavy.

His father, the King, had already affianced him to the Princess of Turan, who would arrive in Samarkand within a month for the marriage. The Princess of Turan was bad-tempered, but she was the richest princess in the East, and his marriage to her would bring wealth and prosperity to Samarkand.

For many nights, the Prince remained awake until midnight, and each night Pari came out and ate his supper. He began to order rare delicacies from the palace kitchen – thrushes' tongues and turtle eggs from the sands of the Nile, all seasoned with spices from the Spice Islands. He grew angry when such rarities could not be found instantly. All through the palace people began to say, 'How difficult the Prince has become. He has fallen in love with his stomach.'

Then, one night, the Prince placed his ring beside his supper plate. At midnight, Pari crept as usual from the trunk of the golden candelabra and went to the table. The Prince stepped out from behind the curtains.

'Have no fear,' he said. 'No harm shall come to you.'

His face was so kind and his voice so gentle that Pari was not frightened. The Prince came and sat beside her at the table and they ate the supper together side by side, while Pari told him her story. When she had finished, the Prince said, 'I have loved you since the first night I saw you, but, alas, I am to marry the bad-tempered Princess of Turan. The wedding feast will be celebrated next week.'

Pari wept and said, 'It was my wish to see the great world. But now I wish to see no more. I shall return to my father in Nishapour.'

'Do not desert me,' cried the Prince, pressing her hands. He placed his ring upon her finger and said, 'With this ring I shall wed thee. Do not doubt me and all will be well.'

So, Pari returned at dawn to her hiding place within the golden trunk. Next day, the Prince said to his father, the King, 'Sire, I do not wish to marry the Princess of Turan. She is bad-tempered and has an evil heart.'

But the King said, 'She has done nothing wrong to you, my son. It is true that people say she is bad-tempered, but wait. Soon the Princess will arrive from Turan. Then you will see that she is as beautiful as a star.'

For another week, Pari lived inside the golden candelabra during the day and at night she shared the Prince's supper with him. They talked and laughed and were happy, and did not think of tomorrow.

But the day arrived, at last, when the gorgeous caravan of the Princess of Turan entered the gates of Samarkand. A parade passed out through the gates in her honour and the Grand Vizier rode on a black horse to welcome her. She was given a suite of rooms in the palace, and the King himself invited her to a midnight feast.

But the Prince was absent from the feast, for he was in his chamber eating apples with Pari.

The Princess of Turan, who was very beautiful but whose heart was black, said to the King, 'Where is my betrothed?'

The King said, 'You will meet him in good time, my lady.'

The Princess of Turan was angry, but she hid her bad temper. She excused herself early from the feast and went to her rooms. There she called her slave-girl. 'Go through all the palace,' she commanded. 'Find where the Prince is and why he failed to receive me.'

The slave-girl walked through the hallways of the palace, listening and watching. When she came to the Prince's door, she asked the guard, 'Where is your master, the Prince?'

'He is inside this room taking supper with his beloved,' the guard answered.

'Who is his beloved?'

'No one knows. By day she vanishes, by night she appears.'

The slave-girl returned to her mistress and told her what she had learned. Then the Princess of Turan ordered the slave-girl to change clothes with her. Dressed as a slave, with her face veiled, the Princess of Turan went to the Prince's door. The guard was fast asleep on the floor, so the Princess peeped through the keyhole. She saw the Prince and Pari laughing together. Fire and rage consumed her heart and she waited there until dawn came. She saw Pari disappear within the trunk of the golden candelabra and she saw the Prince retire to his bed.

When she was sure the Prince was asleep, the Princess of Turan softly opened the door of his chamber and entered. Taking a torch from the fireside, she carefully lighted the one hundred candles of the golden candelabra. Soon the room was blazing with light. The heat from the hundred candles began to warm the golden trunk of the candelabra. Soon it was as hot as fire.

Pari, who was asleep inside, woke with a terrible feeling of being roasted. She could not breathe. She thrust open the door and fell on to the floor in a faint.

The Princess of Turan ran to the guard, shook him awake, and whispered, 'An evil fairy has bewitched this room. I have saved your master, the Prince, from her evil magic. Come quickly and take her away, but do not wake your master.'

The guard ran into the room, wrapped Pari in a rug and, thinking she was dead, threw her into the river which flowed past the castle wall.

The cold water revived Pari and she began to struggle. The swift-flowing water carried her downstream, where an old fisherman sat on the riverbank netting fish. He saw her, threw out his net, and dragged her to shore. Then he carried her to his hut, put her on his straw pallet, and fed her on warm sheep's milk.

When Pari opened her eyes, the old fisherman said, 'Pretty maiden, where is your home?'

Pari answered, 'My home is in the golden candelabra.'

The fisherman said, 'Where is the golden candelabra?'

'Alas,' said Pari, 'I do not know.'

So the fisherman said, 'I am without wife to warm me or child to help me in my labours. You shall stay with me and be my daughter until you find your home again in the golden candelabra.'

So Pari remained with the fisherman in his little hut. She cooked for him and sewed for him and helped him mend his nets. One day, the fisherman came home from the river and said, 'My daughter, the town crier is calling through Samarkand. Our beloved Prince is sick. He refuses to eat. The most expensive meals are prepared for him, but he will not eat them, though only a short while ago he was supping on thrushes' tongues and turtle eggs from the sands of the Nile. He is growing thin and sickly and this is not right, for he is to be married to the Princess of Turan.'

Pari said nothing, but her heart was sore, for now she knew that her golden candelabra had been in the chamber of the Prince of Samarkand, and that he was lost to her for ever.

The fisherman went on, 'The town crier has asked that every cook throughout the countryside prepare a dish to tempt the Prince's appetite. All the women are taking food to the palace and each dish is set before the Prince. Let us hope that something tempts him to eat and get well again.'

Pari said, 'I, too, shall prepare a dish for the Prince. I shall prepare a bowl of brown broth.'

The fisherman was dismayed, for he thought that peasant broth in an earthen bowl would not be accepted by the Prince. But, as he loved Pari, he agreed to take her broth to the palace. Pari cooked some lamb bones with yellow peas and onions and garlic until the broth was rich and brown. Then she poured it into a covered bowl so it wouldn't get cold. When the old fisherman was not looking, she took the Prince's ring from her finger and dropped it into the broth. Then she gave the bowl to the fisherman.

He carried it to the palace, where the guard halted him. 'I have brought a dish to tempt the Prince,' the fisherman said.

'What do you have?' asked the guard and he lifted the cover of the earthen bowl. 'Ugh!' he said. 'Peasant's brown broth! Do you think our Prince, who can't bear to eat thrushes' tongues, will be tempted by your crude brown broth?'

'It is from the hands of a girl nobody knows. She came to me from a golden candelabra,' the fisherman said, so the guard let him pass.

The fisherman walked up the carriageway and through the great marble arch into the palace. At last, he was led to the Prince's chamber. There sat the Prince, pale and wan. Around him on a dozen tables were silver salvers bearing spicy, steaming dishes – plates of lobster-tails and peahens roasted in pomegranate juice and fish from the north sea simmered in ass's milk. But the Prince sat staring at the golden candelabra and eating nothing.

'Great Prince,' said the fisherman, 'may I offer a bowl of brown broth made by the hands of a maiden?'

The Prince looked at him and listened to his humble words. He took the earthen bowl of brown broth and lifted the cover. The broth smelled so good that he dipped in his spoon. He smiled as he tasted the broth and he began to eat.

At the bottom of the bowl, he discovered his own ring. 'Old man,' he cried, 'who has prepared this broth?'

'My daughter has prepared it,' the fisherman said. He was frightened and hung his head.

The Prince commanded in a stern voice, 'Bring your daughter before me at once.'

The old fisherman hurried away, half dead with fear. He ran home and said to Pari, 'My daughter, you must run away, you must leave this town at once. The Prince ate your broth and as he came to the last bite, he grew angry. His eyes flashed fire.'

'Where shall I go?' asked Pari.

The old fisherman said, 'You must follow your destiny. I shall roll you again into the rug and throw you again into the river. I broke the thread of your destiny when I took you out of the river, and now we shall both be punished.'

The old fisherman ran to get the rug, but just then there was a hammering on the door of the hut. The Prince's guards entered and took out their swords and barred the door. Then they marched Pari and the old fisherman to the palace. Pari was trembling with fear, for she did not know why the Prince had been angry when he found her ring at the bottom of the broth. 'He has forgotten me,' she told herself.

When the fisherman and Pari were led into the Prince's chamber, the fisherman threw himself on the floor and begged for mercy. But the Prince had already jumped up from his throne. He ran across the room and knelt at Pari's feet. Everyone was astonished to see the Prince of Samarkand on his knees before a humble fishermaiden.

Then the Prince rose and led Pari to a chair. He said to the old fisherman, 'Forgive me, ancient fisherman. I thought you had stolen the ring which I found in the broth. Rise, and you shall be rewarded, for you have brought me my beloved.'

So Pari and the Prince found each other again, and when Pari told her story to the King, the Princess of Turan was sent back home in disgrace.

Pari married the Prince and invited her own father from Nishapour to the wedding. At the wedding feast, every guest had a bowl of brown broth made by Pari herself. And the golden candelabra always stood in their chamber and brought them good fortune for the rest of their lives.

Arion and the Dolphin

a legend from Ancient Greece
retold by Norah Montgomerie

There was once a musician called Arion, who wandered about the country singing songs, and wherever he sang people stopped to listen.

When the King of Corinth heard his music he invited Arion to live with him in the Royal Palace.

One day Arion received an invitation to compete at the music festival in Sicily.

'You must go,' said the king, 'for I am sure you will win the competition, and the prize is a bag of gold.'

'The gold does not interest me,' said Arion, 'but I would like to compete and of course I would like to win!'

'You may go in one of my ships,' said the king, 'but promise you'll return, for I shall miss your music.'

Arion promised to return, and away he sailed in the king's ship over the sea to the island of Sicily.

All the best musicians in the world were there to compete. One by one they played their instruments and sang their songs, and then it was Arion's turn. He sang so beautifully that the King of Sicily awarded him the first prize, a bag of gold, and all his admirers gave him wonderful gifts of jewels and other treasure. They tried to persuade him to stay on in Sicily, but Arion refused.

'I have promised the King of Corinth I shall return,' said he, 'and his ship waits there in the harbour to carry me home.'

So the King of Sicily and all Arion's friends and admirers saw him off and waved him farewell.

Arion stood on the prow waving to them until they were out

of sight, but when he turned to go to the cabin, he found himself
surrounded by the captain and an angry crew. They had seen
the gold and treasure Arion had carried on board, and had
plotted among themselves how they would take it from him.

'You must die,' said the captain. 'It is the wish of the entire
crew.'

'Why, what have I done to hurt you?'

'You are too rich,' said the captain.

'Spare my life, and I will give you the bag of gold and all the
other treasures that were given to me,' pleaded Arion.

'No, we cannot do that, for when you reach Corinth you may
change your mind, regret your gift, and make us return it,' said
the captain. 'No, it is too dangerous. You must die!'

'Very well,' said Arion, 'I see that your minds are made up.
But please, grant me my last wish. Allow me to sing one more
song before I die.'

'You may do that,' said the captain, 'if, when the last note has
been sung, you leap overboard into the sea.'

Arion promised to do that and, dressed in his finest clothes,
he stood on the prow of the ship and sang more sweetly than he
had ever sung before. Then he took a great leap into the sea; and
the ship sailed on.

Now, a school of dolphins had gathered round to listen to
Arion's songs, for dolphins are very fond of music. When he

leapt from the ship, one of them swam under him, caught him on its back and saved him from drowning. Then the dolphin swam with Arion on its back and reached Corinth long before the ship.

The king was delighted to see Arion, but when he heard how the ship's crew had treated him he was very angry indeed.

'I am astonished my sailors could behave so badly,' he said.

When at last the ship arrived in port, the king sent for the crew.

'Where is Arion?' he asked, pretending he did not know.

'He stayed in Sicily,' said those rascals. 'He was enjoying himself so much he refused to return with us, although we waited several days for him.'

'Is that so?' said the king, frowning with anger.

Then Arion himself came into the room. He was wearing the same clothes in which he had leapt from the ship and, when they saw him, the captain and the crew were terrified.

'A ghost! A ghost!' they cried out. 'Arion was drowned and this must be his ghost!' And in their fright they confessed to the king all that they had done to Arion. The king punished them and ordered them to leave Greece for ever.

As for Arion, he stayed at Corinth and became one of the greatest musicians in all Greece.

The Tale of Caliph Stork

an Arabian tale
by Wilhelm Hauff, translated by Stephen Corrin

One fine afternoon the Caliph Chasid of Baghdad was sitting comfortably on his divan. He had had a little sleep, for the day was very hot and now, after his brief nap, he was smiling and cheerful. He was smoking a long rosewood pipe and sipping a little coffee which a slave had poured out for him and now and then, as if to show how much he was enjoying his drink, he would stroke his beard. In short you had only to give a quick glance at the Caliph to see how perfectly happy he was and utterly at peace with the world. This indeed was the right time to approach him for a talk, and so the Grand Vizier, Mansor, would come regularly at this hour for his daily visit. On this particular afternoon he looked unusually thoughtful.

'Why the serious expression?' asked the Caliph, taking the pipe from his lips.

The Grand Vizier folded his arms and bowed low before the Caliph before replying. 'Sire, I was not aware that I was wearing such a serious expression, but what I do know is that down there near the castle is a pedlar who has a supply of such beautiful goods to sell that I feel annoyed at not having an abundance of money to spend on them.'

Now the Caliph had for some time been wanting to show his Grand Vizier how high in his favour he held him, so he sent one of his slaves to fetch the pedlar to him. Very soon they were both in the Caliph's presence; the pedlar was a short, thick-set man, shabbily dressed, and he carried a small chest with all sorts of wares – beads, rings, lavishly-mounted pistols, goblets and combs. The Caliph and his Vizier examined all the articles very closely, and finally the Caliph bought some beautiful pistols for himself and Mansor and a fine comb for Mansor's wife. When the pedlar was about to close up his chest the Caliph spotted a little drawer and asked whether there were any more things there for sale. The pedlar pulled the drawer out and pointed out a small box containing some blackish-looking powder, and a paper covered with curious writing which neither the Caliph nor his Vizier could make out.

'I got these two things from a merchant who found them in a street in Mecca,' said the pedlar. 'I don't rightly know what they are worth and I'll willingly let you have them for a small price, as they are of no use to me.'

The Caliph, who liked to boast of old manuscripts in his library, although he could not read them himself, bought both the small box and the paper and then dismissed the pedlar. The Caliph, being curious about what the strange-looking writing meant, asked the Vizier if he knew of anyone who might decipher it.

'Most gracious Lord and Master,' replied the latter, 'in the Mosque lives a man called Selim the Scholar who knows all languages. Send for him, for he will surely understand the meaning of these mysterious characters.'

The learned Selim was soon brought into the presence of the Caliph.

'Selim,' said the latter, 'you have the reputation of being a most learned scholar. Have a look at this paper and see if you can understand it. If you can interpret the writing you will be given a new festive robe, but if you cannot you will receive twelve boxes on the ear and twenty-five blows on the soles of your feet, for you will have shown me that you have no reason to be called Selim the Scholar.'

Selim bowed and said, 'Let it be as you command, my Lord.' He examined the paper for some considerable time and then, turning to the Caliph and bowing, he exclaimed, 'If this script is not Latin then let me be hanged!'

'If it indeed be Latin,' said the Caliph, 'then read it to me so that I may understand it.'

Selim began to translate: 'Whoever you are, you who finds this paper, praise Allah for his goodness. Whoever shall take a pinch of the powder in this box and, as he does so, say the word 'MUTABOR', will be able to change himself into any animal he pleases and also understand the language of that animal. When he wishes to resume his human shape he must bow three times towards the east and pronounce that same word. But let him beware of laughing after he has changed his form, for then the enchanted word will disappear from his memory and he will remain an animal.'

The Caliph's delight knew no bounds when he heard all this. He made Selim swear not to reveal the secret to anyone, gave him a splendid robe and dismissed him. 'That is what I would call a good bargain,' he said to his Grand Vizier. 'I am certainly looking forward to changing myself into an animal. Come here early tomorrow morning. We shall go into the fields together, take a pinch of powder out of my box, and listen to everything that is being spoken by living creatures – in the air, in water, in wood and field.'

Hardly had the Caliph breakfasted and dressed the next

morning before the Grand Vizier arrived to accompany him, as commanded, on his walk to the fields. The Caliph stuck the box with the magic powder into his girdle and, ordering his bodyguard to remain behind, set off alone with his Grand Vizier. They passed through the Caliph's extensive gardens and looked about for any creature on which they could test their magic. But in vain. At last the Vizier proposed that they should proceed a little further, to a pond, where he had often seen many animals, especially storks, which had always aroused his interest by their very solemn behaviour and constant chatter. The Caliph agreed and off they went to the pond. As they drew near they saw a stork walking solemnly up and down, looking for frogs and chattering loudly to himself. At the same time they could see another stork, high up in the skies and now flying down to the same spot.

'I'll wager my beard, my Lord,' said the Grand Vizier, 'that these two long-legs are at this very moment about to hold a long conversation with one another. How about turning ourselves into storks?'

'Well spoken!' replied the Caliph, 'but before we do so let us go over what we have to do in order to become men again. Yes, this is it, we bow three times to the east and say 'MUTABOR'. I then become Caliph again and you Grand Vizier. But for heaven's sake, let us remember not to laugh or we are finished!'

As he spoke he saw the other stork hovering above them and slowly coming down to earth. The Caliph quickly drew out the box from his girdle, took a good pinch of powder and handed it to his Vizier, who did likewise. Then they both called out, 'MUTABOR!' Their legs immediately began to shrink and become thin and red; the Caliph's beautiful yellow slippers and those of his companion turned into not very beautiful stork's feet, their arms became wings and their necks stretched out to almost a yard long, their beards vanished and their bodies were covered with soft feathers.

'You've got yourself a pretty beak and no mistake,' said the Caliph to his Grand Vizier after gazing at him in astonishment for a long while. 'By the beard of the Prophet, I have never in my life seen anything like it!'

'My most humble thanks,' replied the Vizier with a low bow, 'but if I may be allowed to say so, I would observe that your Highness looks even more handsome as a stork than as a Caliph – if, of course, that were possible. But, if it please your Highness, let us go and listen to our fellow-storks to see if we really understand their language.'

The stork who had just landed was in the meantime trimming his toes with his beak and preening his feathers. Then he tripped up to the first stork. Our two new storks hurried to get near them and overheard, to their great surprise, the following conversation:

'Good morning to you, Mrs Longleg. Out so early in the meadow?'

'Many thanks, my dear Clapperbeak! I've brought along a small breakfast. Would you care, perhaps, for a small portion of lizard or frog's leg?'

'I thank you humbly, but I don't seem to have any appetite this morning. However, it was for quite another reason that I came into the meadow, for today I am to dance in front of my father's guests and I thought I would be able to get a little quiet practice here.'

Then, as though to encourage him, the young lady stork began to trip daintily amid the grass, executing the most extraordinary movements. The Caliph and Mansor looked on in wonder, and when at last she posed in an artistically picturesque attitude, standing on one foot and at the same time gracefully flapping her wings, they could neither of them restrain their amusement any longer and they burst into uncontrollable laughter. Recovering himself after a while, the Caliph was the first to speak. 'That was indeed a priceless performance. What a shame that our laughter has scared away the silly creatures, or they would most certainly have continued to provide us with more entertainment.'

But then the Vizier suddenly remembered that laughter was forbidden while they were in their changed shape. He was alarmed, and he reminded the Caliph of the prohibition.

'By Mecca and Medina!' exclaimed the latter. 'It's going to be a pretty joke if I have to remain a stork for the rest of my days. Do try and remember that wretched word! I cannot for the life of me think what it was.'

'I remember that we are to bow three times towards the east,' said the Grand Vizier, 'and then say 'Mu – Mu – Mu—. . .'

They both turned towards the east and went on bowing till their beaks nearly touched the ground. But alas! the magic word had completely vanished from their memory, and much as the Caliph kept bowing and much as the Vizier kept desperately calling, 'Mu – Mu –,' no further recollection of it would come back to them. Caliph Chasid and his Grand Vizier Mansor were storks – and that was that.

Sadly the two bewitched men wandered through the fields, not knowing how to cope with their embarrassing situation. They could not get out of their stork skins nor dared they go back into town to make themselves known, for who would believe a stork who claimed to be the Caliph, and even if he were believed would the people of Baghdad accept a stork as their ruler?

So they crept about for several days, feeding on scraps of wild fruit as well as they could, for their long beaks made things rather difficult. They had no appetite at all for frogs and lizards,

169

for they were afraid they might harm their stomachs with such delicacies. Their only pleasure in their miserable state was that they could fly, and so they often flew over the roofs of Baghdad to see what was happening there.

In the first few days they saw signs of great unrest and distress in the streets, but about the fourth day, as they were sitting on the roof of the Caliph's palace, they beheld a magnificent procession down in the street below them. There were drums and fifes, and a man in a scarlet, gold-embroidered cloak rode along on a colourfully decorated horse. Richly dressed attendants accompanied him and half Baghdad came following behind, crying, 'Hail Mirza! Hail to the Lord of Baghdad!'

The two storks on the palace roof glanced at one another.

'Can you guess what suspicion has entered my mind, Grand Vizier?' asked the Caliph. 'Can you see now why I was put under this spell? This man Mirza is the son of my sworn enemy, the powerful sorcerer Kaschnur, who has sworn to take vengeance on me. But I am not giving up hope yet. Come with me, faithful companion of my misfortune, and we will make our way to the tomb of the Prophet. At that holy place maybe we shall be freed from this spell.'

They flew up from the Palace roof and made for the direction of Medina. It was by no means easy for them, for neither had had much practice at flying. 'Oh, my gracious Lord,' groaned the Vizier after they had been going for a couple of hours, 'with your leave I must say that I cannot hold out much longer; you are flying too quickly for me. Besides, dusk is already closing in and we would be well advised to seek shelter for the night.'

Caliph Chasid agreed to his companion's request. In the valley below he caught sight of a ruined building which seemed to promise them a night's shelter, and they directed their flight there. The place where they were now about to settle down for the night seemed to be the remains of an old castle. Splendid pillars stood out among the ruins, and several rooms which were still in good condition were evidence of the onetime splendour of the building. Chasid and his companion walked up and down the passages to find some dry spot for themselves. Suddenly stork Mansor stood stock still. 'My Lord and Master,' he whispered, 'if it were not just too ridiculous for a Grand Vizier, and perhaps even more for a stork, to be frightened of ghosts, I should feel quite uncomfortable and somewhat alarmed, for I distinctly caught the sound of sighing and moaning close by.' At these words the Caliph also stood still, and he too could hear a low moaning that seemed to come from a human being rather than from an animal. Full of curious expectation, the Caliph was eager to move towards the corner from which the sounds seemed to come, but his Vizier caught hold of his wing with his beak and begged him urgently not rush into new and unknown dangers. But it was no use. The Caliph, beneath whose stork's wings there still beat a brave heart, tore himself away with the loss of a few feathers and hurried along into a dark passage. He soon came to a door, apparently only on the latch, and hearing unmistakable sighs and groans, pushed it open with his beak – then paused on the threshold in utter amazement. There on the floor of the dilapidated room, dimly lit by a small grated window, sat a large screech-owl. Big tears rolled from her great

round eyes and hoarse cries of distress came from her hooked beak. But when she caught sight of the Caliph and his Vizier, who had followed him, she gave a shriek of joy. Gracefully she wiped away the tears with her brown flecked wings and, to the utter astonishment of the two visitors, she called out, in excellent Arabic, and in a human voice, 'Welcome, welcome, storks!

In you I see the sign of my rescue, for it was once prophesied to me that great happiness would be mine from a visit of storks!'

When the Caliph had recovered from his astonishment, he bowed to the owl with his long neck and, arranging his thin legs in a fittingly graceful stance, said, 'Owl, your words allow me to suspect that we have found in you a companion in misfortune. But, alas! your hope of obtaining freedom through us is a vain one. You will readily understand our helplessness when you have heard our story.' The owl begged him to tell her all and the Caliph thereupon recounted the events we already know.

When the Caliph had completed his story the owl thanked him and said, 'Now, if you please, you must listen to my tale and you will see that I am no less unfortunate than you are. 'My father is the King of India and I, his only unhappy daughter, am called Lusa. The evil magician Kaschnur, who bewitched you, has also plunged me into this wretched state. He came one day to my father's palace and asked that I be given as wife to his son Mirza. My father, a hot-tempered man, had him thrown downstairs. The vile enchanter, however, found ways of approaching me disguised in another form, and one day when I had gone into my garden to take some refreshment, he came to me dressed as a slave and brought me a drink which changed me into the hideous shape in which you now see me. As he carried me, helpless with fear, to this place, he shouted into my ear in a terrible voice, 'Here you will remain, ugly creature, an object of ridicule even to animals, till the end of your life or until someone, of his own free will, asks you to be his wife even in the repulsive shape you now wear. Thus do I take my revenge on you and your arrogant father.' Since that fateful day many, many months have passed. Wretchedly sad and lonely, I spend my days within these walls like a hermit, shunned by the world and despised by animals. The beauties of Nature are hidden from me, for I am blind by day and the veil falls from before my eyes only when the moon sheds her wan light upon these ruins.'

The owl had ended her tale and once more wiped her eyes

with her wing; telling her grim story had been too much for her.

As he listened to the Princess's tale the Caliph became sunk in deep thought. 'I may be deluding myself,' he said, 'but I think I see some secret connection between our misfortunes. But where shall we find the key to this mystery?'

'I, too, suspect this,' replied the owl, 'for when I was a child a wise woman foretold that one day a stork would bring me some great happiness, and now it seems to me possible that I may have the knowledge whereby we can get ourselves free.'

The Caliph, much surprised at hearing this, asked her what she meant. 'Once a month,' explained the owl, 'the sorcerer who has cast this misfortune upon us both pays a visit to these ruins. Not very far from this room there is a dining-hall where he and several of his companions come regularly to feast and drink. I have often overheard them there, recounting the shameful things they have done. Perhaps – who knows? – he might let out the magic word which you cannot remember.'

'My dear Princess,' exclaimed the Caliph, 'tell me, please, when does he come, and where is the dining-hall?'

The owl was silent for a few moments. Then she said, 'Don't think badly of me, but only on one condition can I reveal to you what you ask.'

'Speak! Speak!' cried the Caliph. 'Command and I am ready to agree to anything you ask!'

'I will speak,' said the Princess. 'Naturally I too wish to be freed as quickly as possible, but this can happen only if one of you will offer me his hand.'

Both storks were taken aback by this proposal and the Caliph beckoned to his Vizier to go outside for a moment.

'Grand Vizier,' said the Caliph, 'this is turning out to be a very odd sort of affair . . . perhaps . . . you could take her.'

'Indeed!' exclaimed the latter. 'And risk having my eyes torn out by my wife when I get home! Furthermore, I am an old man, while you are young and unmarried. You are therefore a more suitable match for a young and beautiful princess.'

'That is just the point,' sighed the Caliph, his wings drooping sadly as he spoke. 'Who says she is young and beautiful? It's like buying a pig in a poke.'

They went on arguing for some time, but at last the Caliph, seeing that his Grand Vizier would rather remain a stork than marry an owl, decided that he would have to be the one to accept the Princess's condition. When they went in and told her, she was overcome with joy. They could not have chosen a better time to come, she told them, for the magicians would most likely hold their meeting that very night.

She then led the storks out of the room to show them the way to the dining-hall. They walked for some way along a dark passage. At last they met a bright beam of light streaming through a partly ruined wall. The owl told them to stand quite still and peer through the gap, and they were able to see right into the large hall. All around it were pillars, lavishly adorned; coloured lamps made it as light as day, and in the middle of the hall stood a table laden with the choicest dishes and surrounded by a sofa on which eight men were seated. The storks recognized one of them as the pedlar who had sold them the magic powder. The man next to him asked him to tell of his latest feats. And among his tales was that of the Caliph and his Grand Vizier!

'What was the word you gave them?' asked another of the magicians.

'A good, solid Latin word – MUTABOR.'

When the storks overheard this through the gap in the wall, they could not restrain their joy. They started to run so fast on their long legs towards the door of the ruin that the owl could scarcely keep up with them. At the door the Caliph turned to her and with great emotion said, 'Saviour of my life and the life of my friend, as a token of my eternal gratitude for what you have done, I beg you to accept me as your husband.' Then he turned towards the east, and both storks bent their long necks three times towards the sun which was at that moment rising from behind the mountains. 'MUTABOR!' they both cried and in a trice they were changed into their former human selves, and in their great joy fell laughing and weeping into each other's arms. But who can describe their astonishment when they

looked round! Before them stood a most beautiful lady, magnificently dressed, who smilingly held out her hand to the Caliph. 'Do you no longer recognize your owl?' she asked. For it was indeed she. The Caliph was so entranced with her beauty and sweetness that he exclaimed that the luckiest thing that ever happened to him was being turned into a stork.

The three of them now made their way together to Baghdad. In his clothes the Caliph found not only the little box of powder but also his purse, so in the first village they came to he was able to buy everything they needed for their journey. Before long they arrived at the gates of Baghdad. The sight of the Caliph caused the wildest astonishment in the town, for he had been given up as dead. There was therefore great rejoicing when it was realized that their beloved ruler was back among them again. And all the more fiercely did their anger and hatred burn against the traitor Mirza. They made their way to the Palace and took the old magician prisoner. The Caliph ordered the old man to be sent to the room in the ruined building in which the Princess had spent her days as an owl, there to remain for the rest of his life. Mirza was sentenced to life imprisonment.

Imagine that!

Caliph Chasid and his wife lived long and happily together. His most delightful hours were always those when the Grand Vizier came to pay him his regular afternoon visit. Then they would talk of their 'stork adventure' and if the Caliph was in more than usually good spirits he would even deign to imitate what the Grand Vizier looked like when he was a stork. He would stalk solemnly up and down the room, his feet stiffly splayed, waving his arms as if they were wings and, with his face turned towards the east, cry out in vain, 'Mu – Mu.' This performance was a constant source of delight for the Princess and her children, but if the Caliph went on too long, clattering and bowing and crying, 'Mu— Mu—', the Vizier would threaten to tell the Caliph's wife all about the discussion they had had on that fateful night outside the owl-Princess's door. And that was a sure way of putting a stop to the Caliph's little frolic!